Afentis Batistas

Costas Montis

Afentis Batistas

A Novel

Translated by
Stalo Monti-Pouagare

Feather Star Publishing
Dayton, Ohio

Feather Star Publishing
P.O. Box 752126
Dayton, OH 45475-2126
www.featherstarpublishing.com

Published January 2006

ISBN 0-9773769-0-7

Library of Congress Control Number: 2005933958

Originally published in Greek as *Ο αφέντης Μπατίστας και τ'άλλα*
Hermes, Athens, 1980

Cover: Lorenzo Lotto, Italian, 1480-1556. *Portrait of a man*, c. 1525.
Oil on canvas, 108.2 x 100.5cm. © The Cleveland Museum of Art,
Gift of the Hanna Fund, 1950.250
Reproduced by permission

Printed in the U.S.A. by
Morris Publishing
3212 East Highway 30
Kearney, NE 68847
1-800-650-7888

This book is printed on acid-free paper.

In loving memory of my father

Stalo

Even though afentis Batistas may not be the main character of the narration—nor do I know anymore whether there is a main character—, even though, while I was looking for him, other things may have surfaced, just as when we pick a cherry and ten more are pulled up with it, even though I may have been looking exactly for the other things that surfaced, even though other things may have been the important ones and afentis Batistas was just a pretext, mine or I don't know whose, in any case, he first, at least seemingly and with so much persistence at that, set the ball rolling.

My acquaintance with him started with grandmother's stories. The more vaguely and incorporeally I remember grandmother, the more alive her fairy tales, her songs, and, most of all, her stories about the "afentis," her strange great grandfather, have remained. I understand, of course, why and how everything has been imprinted so indelibly inside me, how everything has been kneaded and withstood time, but it is strange that, in addition to that, I remember all the other things associated with grandmother except her, as if those things absorbed her, as if she were dispersed in them and erased. So much so that I'm afraid that I would not recognize her if she happened to pass by my street on a Sunday morning coming out of church with other women ("Your grandmother was among them." "My grandmother? Which one was she?"). And it is also strange that I have never had any questions, that I keep passing all of them by, and when I remember grandmother, I have no questions, I am completely satisfied with what I see, without seeing

1

almost anything in the established way. (Grandmother. Nothing else. That's enough.)

Her room, a small mezzanine, was at the end of a long and narrow corridor, right where we turned to go to our own rooms. Going in and out of the house, we would pass in front of its wooden staircase and, without seeing grandmother, we would greet her, just as the women in the villages cross themselves when they pass by a church, even if they cannot see it.

"Good morning, grandmother. Good evening, grandmother. Goodnight, grandmother. How are you, grandmother?"

Our greeting at the turn of the corridor would come out automatic, spontaneous, and often colorless and absent-minded, regardless of whatever else occupied our minds. And the reply would be heard feeble, faded, which most times could not reach us, which we would not even in the slightest slow down to wait for. And it seemed as if it were coming from a different world. After all, we did consider grandmother a different world. On this side all of us, on that side grandmother.

"Good morning, my child. Be well, my child. God and the Holy Mary bless you, my child."

Father and mother would make more conversation.

"How is it going, old gal?"

"Did you sleep well, mother? How is your leg?"

"I'm okay, son. My leg is just fine today."

From the time that my memories begin, grandmother lived with us. We considered her an inseparable member of the family, even as she worried that she was a burden to us. She would say that to father, and father would scold her.

"I'm hung on to you like a bunch of grapes."

"What are you talking about, for God's sake?"

I cannot tell from which stories, hers or later mother's, we knew about the great poverty that she had been through. We even knew then, or found out later (the origins, the dates, our own processes and additions are confused), about the romance of father with mother. He would start from Nicosia, so the story goes, or even

2

from his village, Lapithos, on the northern coast of the island, riding on his horse, "Hasamboulis," to go to Famagusta, seventy miles away, to see the shy, pale girl he was in love with, the fallen noble girl with the big, "bee-patterned" eyes and the Venetian family name.

He would pass by the seamstress shop of her forewoman. Tak, tak, tak, sounded the horse on the pavement. Tak, tak, tak, like a signal and like a serenade ("Open the window, open the crystal pane," something like that).

The apprentice girls would recognize the "tak-tak" and run.

"Girls, it's 'you-know-who'!"

"Hey, Kalomoira, get the scarf!"

It was a variety in their monotonous, secluded life. They were coming and going to the window letting out joyful sounds.

"Hey, you! Hey, rider!"

And they would run inside with drowned laughs.

Only Maroula would not run inside, and she would stay there and chat with him:

"She is here. She is shy of you and hiding. What can you do? You chose our shy one!"

My father would say something, and Maroula was always there. And she was beautiful too, she was beautiful like fire.

"Did you hear what she said? She will take him from you," the others stung mother.

"You should see how handsome he is today! A captain! Come out, then; he will melt with love! Wax will be dripping from the horse, I'm telling you. Don't you have a heart?"

The teasings of the girls might also include a flower that they, unseen, would throw to the street.

"From your Kalomoira!"

And sometimes it was not just one flower. Soon another followed and another. And father would say:

"That's enough tell her. She has loaded me!"

As time went by and my mother would not go to the window, the others would lift her and manage to show her off:

"Here she is!"

The kind-hearted forewoman was amused and did not interfere. After all, the arrival of the love-stricken rider was a pleasant variety in her life too. She would simply say:

"It's a good thing that the neighborhood is out of the way."

He was fifteen years older than my mother, and grandmother would hesitate:

"I will treat her like a queen, kyra-Eleni. Don't you see that she is withered from poverty? She will die on you."

"Don't say such a word, son, please. I don't know what to do. There is such a big age difference. Even the church won't give permission."

Indeed, the church did not give permission in such cases, but the following week father brought the papers from the archbishopric. He took them to the forewoman with gifts and embroideries from Lapithos. And the forewoman talked it over again with kyra-Eleni.

We lived at the time in Skala—Larnaca, as it was labeled on the map—and I must have been about four years old when the story begins, the youngest of the six children buzzing in the house. I was grandmother's most frequent visitor. I would go slowly and broadly, like splashing in the water, up the steps that led to her seclusion, the seclusion that she herself had chosen.

"I like it here, so isolated and quiet, my daughter," she would tell mother.

"And the staircase?"

"It's only six steps. I'll be going up slowly."

Have you ever noticed how little children tread on the last step, with how much victory, with how much full stop, with how much end, with how much "we're here"? (Like that, plural, "we're here." The plural is important.) Many times later, I envied that old arriving of mine, many times I longed for it, many times I looked for it in a thousand other cases when I would arrive and not arrive, when I would start for grandmother's mezzanine and there was no mezzanine, and there was not even an indication and there was no breath and there was no grandmother or fairy tale waiting for me ("Grandmother? What grandmother? We didn't hear. Fairy tale? What fairy tale? We didn't hear. Wrong").

"Hello, grandmother!"

Just like climbing up and pinning your flag in the fortress, like "we've won" in Athens, which is anxiously waiting for news.

We would sit down so that she could tell us the fairy tales about the "Green-headed Bird" and the "Myrsinokokkos" or the songs about "Arodafnousa" and "Lygeri and the King":

Up in the upper neighborhood, the upper and the lower,
A pretty girl is perishing from bitter, hopeless love.

And we would sit down so that she could also tell us about "afentis Batistas." We could tell, I think, that she liked to dig up the stories about her great grandfather, maybe because they brought to life events from the time when she was not poor and hanging from father's charity. Besides, we wanted nothing more than the stories about the "afentis."

I was, as I said, grandmother's most frequent visitor and the most loyal. While my brothers and sisters were growing up and making absences or, one by one, staying away from the mezzanine altogether, I remained. Plaf, plaf, plaf, the splashing on the wooden staircase and plaf the arriving and the pinning of the flag.

"Hello, grandmother!"

She would open her arms for me and reply with a distich:

Welcome, my dear and tireless ears, welcome, voracious ears,
Welcome, beloved eyes of eyes, come here and bring me cheers.

Sometimes she would say the first line and let me struggle over the second one. Or she would say one or two words and stop so that

I could complete it, then another one or two, and another one or two.

Unfortunately, grandmother did not wait for me to grow up so that I could prove that I would not stop going like the others, even though the continuation that I later gave to the memories of my childhood associations with her showed clearly that at least it would be a long time before I would start my infidelities.

I would even feel embittered and hurt if later, whenever we remembered grandmother, one of my brothers or sisters happened to remark thoughtlessly and with the arrogance of first knowledge:

"Grandmother used to exaggerate a little bit."

No, she did not exaggerate, she did not exaggerate at all. After all, so what if she exaggerated? Even now, especially now, come, grandmother, and exaggerate, come back, grandmother, and exaggerate.

So much did grandmother not wait for me to grow up, so much did I not have time to grow up, that she left before I even had the curiosity to ask her if the distich with which she replied to my greeting was hers.

And I would ask her even more:

"Did you make up any more, grandmother?"

And maybe she would answer:

"No. I made up one and only one. For you."

Grandmother's narrations were taking on different dimensions inside me as I was growing up, they would stop being nuclei and seeds, they would sprout, expand by themselves, complete themselves, interpret themselves, and as such will I try to present them.

The introduction to afentis Batistas was the episode with the safe. Grandmother must have given it priority, because, even as it confirmed her old rich roots to us, at the same time it established the "afentis" in our childhood feelings, securing him a spectacular entrance.

The afentis, she said, had one day forgotten his safe open. Grandmother saw it overflowing with golden glittering liras, and she got scared and ran to him gaspingly.

"Afentis grandfather, the safe is open."

The afentis is not worried. He is playing with her.

"Oh really?"

"Yes, grandfather, I'm telling you!"

"Wide open?"

"Wide open. The golden liras are showing."

"The golden liras are showing?"

"Yes, grandfather, I saw them. Run!"

"Okay, I'm going."

"Do you want me to run in front?"

"No, don't run in front. And don't gasp either."

Why did she gasp anyway? If she could understand, he would tell her not to let the golden liras see such gasping and mock and put on airs ("First, calm down").

He took her by the hand.

("Let's go.")

The safe was indeed wide open showing its gold to the sun that filled the room, showing the sun to its gold.

"So, here is the sun I was telling you about. So, here is the gold, which compares to you."

A bee got in the safe, flew around, buzzed, and left indifferent.

"Bring your little jug," said the afentis to grandmother.

He took handfuls and handfuls of golden liras, like little pebbles from the sea, and filled it up for her.

"Up to the very top, grandmother?"

"Up to the very top."

Perhaps he wanted to tell her again:

"So that you won't be afraid of them. And listen, I don't want you to condescend to put them on as trinkets and necklaces, I don't want you to wear them as bracelets and rings and let them contaminate your little hands. Did you see how the bee turned its back on them?"

7

But he told her other things instead:

"If the safe were not open, how would the golden liras see a bee buzzing?"

Such talk was not for grandmother. She grabbed the little jug, hid it under her apron, and left running as if afraid that grandfather might change his mind. She crossed the estate as if chased, went to a hiding place in the hedge, dug a hole, and hid the little jug in the ground.

"Didn't the afentis ever ask you later what you did with the golden liras?"

"No, never. As if he had forgotten about them."

Even if the afentis had forgotten about them, grandmother would not forget them, and every day she spent a lot of time alone at her hiding place.

"Where were you again?" they would ask her.

"I went for a walk in the estate."

As for us, even though we did not know exactly what money meant beyond its capability to be exchanged with different things at the grocer's and at the baker's, we knew very well the meaning of gold and golden liras, because they were interwoven with fairy tales and their suggestions, and they would enrapture us. Solid gold were the doors of the palace, golden the plates and the utensils of the fairies, from a golden jug did the prince drink water, with golden fans did the nursemaids fan him, in a solid gold bed did he sleep, a golden apple was Arodafnousa holding and playing with (By the way, why do fairy tales so carelessly praise gold to us? Can it be that we have been influenced?).

"You could become a princess, grandmother, if you wanted," I said.

My brothers and sisters laughed.

"Not even Arodafnousa?" I insisted.

More laughs.

Grandmother was describing to us the estate of the afentis in the middle of an endless grove in Ayios Memnon, four miles from

Famagusta, and she was building inside us something like the castles that I later read about in the fairy tales of the north.

And she was telling us about the afentis' hanging mustache, his black Russian hat, his velvet vest with the thick golden chain. Scant, sharp, heavy were his words, as if made of lead that falls and sinks in the water.

She never saw him smile, she said, even when his friend Beneducci came—once in a while—from Skala. He was his only friend, a tall, slender old man, with faded blue eyes, who, unlike the afentis, laughed at the slightest thing. He would stay for a few days at the village, and the two of them would close themselves up for hours, ordering continually coffee and a change for the pipe bowl and the nargiles, the nargiles with the velvet hoses and the daisies on the glass, or they would go out for long walks in the estate. The afentis had no other friend.

In Famagusta he would make his first appearance in October, when the exportation of pomegranates to Misr and Beirut was starting. They would look at him then in his cabriolet carriage like a strange phenomenon.

"Batistas!"

They saw him as an indication that the loading of the pomegranates was starting.

"A caique must have come. Batistas has passed by."

He would cross the market place quickly, without greeting much, as if absorbed in thought. Besides, the truth is that he did not know but the very few people he had dealings with.

He would go straight to the port and up the caiques to chat with the owners, Greeks and Arabs, almost all of whom he knew and entertained at the estate.

Who knows, I was wondering with a dose of romanticism when I started taking notes about Batistas and researching his Venetian origins, what these associations, which were going further than was needed for the loading of his pomegranates, stirred in his subconscious, what ancestral forgotten sea, what old Venice.

I could imagine some conversations:

"You call Misr a trip, captain? You can swim to it. It's just a two-yard lake, a mouthful of sea. Go a little farther away."

Or:

"Your storerooms are fed up with pomegranates, captain. Show them some good merchandise to make them happy."

Or:

"How is the three-mast galley, captain?"

The caique owners welcomed the teasings and would reply in the same tone:

"It's not a galley, joker Batistas. It's a *trechantiri*. You can't tell the boats apart. You're forgetting them."

"The waters of Misr are not a lake, sior Batistas, even if they are just a mouthful. Come with us for a ride and we'll talk again, rather than stay planted like a pomegranate on the shore. What do you say?"

And indeed Batistas went to Misr.

"Okay, captain, I'll go. On your next trip I'll go too so that your sails will swell full!"

Since it was his first time traveling, for a whole month he was planning his return, albeit temporary, to the sea from where his ancestors had sailed as conquerors centuries earlier. For a whole month, the estate was talking about his trip.

"What is the afentis going to do now in Misr?"

"Who knows? Business."

"What business? Unload his pomegranates?"

Even in Famagusta, people heard about it and were surprised.

"Did you hear that Batistas is going on a trip?"

"Why not? The man is a Venetian."

And how he prepared his "return" to the sea! He ordered a navy suit and a cap and boots, he filled a suitcase with all kinds of little gifts for the sailors of the caique and for those he would meet in Misr, and he prepared cases with wines and smoked ham and sausages as if he were going to Venice.

"So that they will always remember and talk about it. So that it will stay in the history of the sea!"

And finally the caique came.

"The caique of the afentis is here!"

Batistas made his usual visit and inspected the loading of the pomegranates.

"Are you ready, sior Batistas? We are leaving tomorrow."

A great day dawned. Early in the morning the people of the estate gathered at the port to bid him goodbye. And Batistas arrived in his cabriolet carriage dressed in his navy uniform. As he was proudly crossing the town, the Famagustans were looking at him with curiosity and surprise.

"Look! He is dressed like a captain."

"He's not in his right mind. He's gone nuts."

On the caique, even though they were surprised, even though they did not expect him to come dressed in a captain's uniform, they kept their cool. As if on cue, they stood in line and saluted him.

"Welcome to your galley, admiral!"

"You will have things to remember and talk about," Batistas replied. "I will exalt you!"

And the caique, loaded with pomegranates, sailed slowly amid the wavings of hands and handkerchiefs.

And someone said:

"The caique of the afentis is pregnant!"

When they sailed into the open sea, the captain, a joker from Rhodes, took out of his bag and unfolded a cloth with two poorly painted lion cubs.

"Shall we raise the flag too, sior Batistas?"

Batistas accepted the joke. And the flag was hoisted on the middle mast with shouts and applause. At first, it could not believe its eyes and stayed for a while distrustful, reluctant, and crumpled. Then, however, it adapted to the situation and fluttered and waved happily its lion cubs in the sea breeze ("Why not?" it seemed to be saying. "Everything is possible in the world").

Batistas was finding an escape from the monotony of Ayios Memnon and was enjoying it. Besides, he himself had started it with the navy uniform that he had put on. He asked the men to open the case with the drinks.

"To the health of Venice!"

The captain knew a song of Napoli and he started singing.

"Your song is not about Venice," noted Batistas, who happened to catch the word "Napoli."

"It doesn't matter," replied the Rhodian, "in times of drought, even hail is welcome!"

The fun continued into the next day until they reached the stormy waters of Alexandria. Batistas remembered the captain's words that the waters of Misr were not a lake. He felt dizzy, nauseated. He was humbled and said it:

"It's nothing, sior Batistas. It's your first time traveling. Go and lie down."

"It's not the sea to blame, it's the drinking," said Batistas.

However much he tried to hold the vomiting, he didn't succeed.

"Not here, farther down so that the flag won't see," said the captain laughing.

Another narration of grandmother's was the story about Katingo and her donkey. Katingo was a poor old maid who worked hard cleaning houses to earn her living. She never complained whatever chore they asked her to do. She would say:

"As long as you don't ask me to nurse a baby!"

She lived all alone in a tumble-down little room in Kato Varosia. Her characteristic was that she always wore shoes with thin high heels. Nobody knew what the high heels reminded her of, nobody knew how she came to love them so much, where her persistent preference stemmed from, and the fashion would come and go, but the thin high heels would always be there, uninfluenced and immovable, in church, in her walks, at work, everywhere, even at home. You might even say that she avoided walking barefoot and resting her feet lest she should be without her heels even for a little while. In the houses where she worked, they knew about this and they would not ask her to take off the high heels. She might be offended and never come back.

She was thin like the heels of her shoes, so skinny that the wind could blow her away while it was caressing her scant, sparse hair. And because of the way she was prancing on her heels and stumbling on an occasional rock on the dirt road, they gave her the nickname "You swagger and prance."

"Tomorrow we will have 'You swagger and prance.'"

Nickname, of course, was just a figure of speech, because the little phrase, which nobody at all shouted at her in her youth and which now the high heels were offering her, was not a nickname.

"You swagger and prance!"

An imperceptible, delayed pleasure would form on her withered face.

One day that Katingo went out for herbs, while crossing the dry bed of the Pedieos river, she saw a bony, half-dead donkey. Someone had most probably abandoned him there to die. Katingo went closer. His ribs were separating, the bones in his buttocks were ready to poke through the skin and come out. He was biting without appetite some dry thistles and was wagging continually his tail and ears to keep away the flies, which had realized how defenseless he was and were attacking. The person who had thrown him away had not even left a bucket of water for him, perhaps to speed up death.

He did not pay any attention to Katingo. The old maid caressed him softly. The donkey turned slowly with extinguished, hazy, plaintive eyes. And that gaze stabbed a knife in her heart.

"They threw you away, eh? Don't worry, I'll take you."

And she took him. She took him and gave him all the affection that was swaddled inside her and which, until now, did not know what direction to take. They would see her dragging him so bony and they would laugh:

"God brought them together. The pot rolled and found its lid."

And the "You swagger and prance" now became plural:

"They swagger and prance."

They would say:

"As long as she doesn't put high horseshoes on the donkey!"

They even made up a tongue twister (God forbid you should incur the gossip of an idle neighborhood):

Up high a high-horseshoer high-horseshoed
The high-horseshoed horse up high!

With care (care for a beloved, long-awaited child), the donkey became alive again, gained strength, found his curves, the bones hid in their failure and postponed the perforation of the skin, nature had second thoughts. Katingo was not jealous that she could not find also her old curves (for she must have had old curves, for all things at some time have curves), and she could not wait to get off work so that she could take her donkey for a walk. They were both walking, just like friends holding hands while coming back from school. It never crossed her mind to ride him.

"Hey fellows, Katingo and her donkey!"

They did not say "Katingo *with* her donkey," they said "Katingo *and* her donkey" mockingly making them equal. And to make it even clearer, they would greet in the plural:

"Hello, you two!"

It was that plural that would get you in big trouble if you used it on someone riding or dragging a donkey. Especially if the greeting were clarified with "fellows" or "gentlemen":

"Hello, fellows! Hello, gentlemen!"

It was, and still is, one of the most dangerous teasings, especially in villages, almost as dangerous as when you drink your coffee at a coffeehouse and you turn the coffee cup over. It is, they say, as if you were making an indecent proposal to the coffeehouse owner. They were telling me about a similar case of a young man and a girl from Limassol, summer tourists in the Marathasa valley, who turned their coffee cups over to read their fortune. The coffeehouse owner, a big man with a thick mustache, tried to control himself and explained phlegmatically and in the form of a joke to the patrons of the coffeehouse:

"The young man's coffee cup evens out with the girl's coffee cup. It's allowed!"

Even though the patrons laughed and seemed to let it pass, they decided to play a prank on him. They talked it over with the young man, and the next day they sent him alone to the coffeehouse.

The owner looked at him suspiciously. Did he, by any chance, come to repeat the proposal? Did he, by any chance, really mean it? He glanced at the patrons as if telling them:

"You are witnesses!"

The young man drank quietly his coffee and turned matter-of-factly the cup over. The owner flared up, blushed, looked at the young man fiercely, and looked at the others, who were watching. Fortunately, he suddenly remembered that they had to treat the tourists well so that the Solea valley would not take them away. He pointed to the young man with contempt:

"Look at that!"

And he showed ingenuity:

"Do you know the joke of Aslani Hodja? One day he was holding a tender, beautiful young boy on his shoulders and was going around the market place. The beautiful boy was shouting at the top of his lungs:

'I seduced Aslani Hodja!'

Instead of replying, the hodja was whispering calmly:

'Whoever has eyes can see!'"

However, in Katingo's case things were different. Katingo was happy both with the "and" and with the plural.

"They threw him away to die and I resurrected him!" she was bragging.

And all of a sudden calamity struck. One day Yiannis Vrakas, the former owner of the donkey, appeared. He had not thrown him away, he said. He had lost him. He also brought a paper from the mayor of the village certifying that the donkey was his.

Katingo cried, begged, shouted:

15

"That's a lie! You threw him away and I picked him up."
To no avail. They took the donkey away from her.
"I'll give you whatever you spent," Vrakas told her.
"I don't want money. He deserved it. It's not on you that I spent it, and you can't give it back to me. I want my donkey."
The owner was heartless. Heartless? Katingo had no room for retreat. She found out that Vrakas worked at the estate, and she went there. She fell at Batistas' feet. She told him everything.
"My afentis, I'm in God's hands and in yours. Without my donkey, I will die."
Batistas listened scowling, without speaking. He sent for Vrakas.
"How much do you want for the donkey?"
"Afentis…."
"Say how much, and I don't want to see you ever again! The estate cannot stand you."
Vrakas was stunned. He thought of being without a job, he thought of losing Batistas forever. He bowed his head.
"I don't want anything, my afentis. I'll give her back the donkey since you are ordering me to. Let her have what's rightfully mine."
"It's not rightfully yours! And next time you have a donkey to throw away, bring him to the estate to spend his old age and don't just leave him on dry river beds. Is that clear? And you come too when you get old!"
It seems that the thought of resorting to Batistas was reinforced in Katingo's mind by the fact that all the people who had extra newborn kittens and puppies that they did not want to keep would throw them away at the estate.
"Put them in a bag and take them to the estate!"
They were welcome there. People did not have to throw them away secretly, as they would if they had a compassionate and sensitive neighbor, in which case they would leave the newborn puppies in his yard or on his doorstep at night and irritate him:
"Who threw them away this time?"

16

"I don't know, I didn't see."

At the estate they were given as if in exercise of a right.

"I've brought some puppies."

The only difference is that they were not asking for a receipt!

And the grove was filling up with cats and dogs, a whole army following Batistas on his walks.

And people would make similes:

"Why did you gather them like Batistas' cats?"

Much later, I adopted the story about the "intellectual." When grandmother was telling us the story, it was received with little interest. First of all, she could not explain what the word "intellectual" meant; it was just not possible for her to explain to us. She would try "a man of letters" and we would ask her "what letters?"

The workers at the estate gave the nickname "intellectual" to Nikodemos, a skinny young man twenty-four, twenty-five years old with sucked-in cheeks. And they called him "intellectual" because of his glasses. Wearing glasses was a rare thing in Cyprus then and even much rarer—almost nonexistent—for a worker, especially a farm worker. Nikodemos was from Karpasi, the poorest area of the island. And he was not at all an intellectual. The man was by heredity extremely nearsighted.

When he first came to the estate for work, they advised him not to appear before Batistas wearing glasses.

"If he sees that you wear glasses, he won't take you."

"What's wrong with wearing glasses?" Nikodemos was wondering.

"You are asking what's wrong? For workers it's just plain wrong."

He followed their advice, and, therefore, he was forced to hide his glasses every time Batistas was coming near. The others would call out to him and have fun:

"Hey, intellectual, the glasses! The boss is coming!"

Nikodemos would rush to put them in his pocket. He would grab them with his dirty hands and make them blurry.

And one day the supervisor whispered the going-ons to Batistas. And to anticipate any good-natured people, he also said that the "intellectual" was not working efficiently.

"Half build, afentis."

"Why did you call him 'intellectual'?" asked Batistas.

"That's what they call him, because of the glasses. It's not bad. He doesn't get mad."

The next morning Batistas went to find Nikodemos. Nikodemos saw him from far away, the others called out to him too, and he hid his glasses.

Batistas came closer.

"Put on your glasses!" he told him. "How come you are like this?"

The "intellectual" was stunned. What was the meaning of how come he was like this? Did he know him any other way? He looked at the other workers as if trying to find the traitor; he was looking plaintively at them as if saying, "Why did you do it?"

"Put on your glasses!" repeated Batistas.

The "intellectual" took his glasses slowly out of his pocket and put them on timidly.

"There," said Batistas. "And when you get tired, just stop working and rest. If you had come from the beginning with your glasses on, I might have made you supervisor. Do you like being nicknamed 'intellectual'?"

"I don't mind," said Nikodemos timidly with a distant, muffled, bony voice.

"He doesn't mind," said the others too.

Grandmother was also telling us about some inexplicable whims of the afentis'. Many times, she said, when it was raining very hard, he would go out and enjoy the rain pounding on him. He would open his hands to grab it, he would open his mouth to drink it, and he would go back to the estate soaking wet.

"Lest the rain should go to waste," he would say. "It's a living thing. Lest it should say that it came and that we hid in the house."

Incomprehensible things to grandmother. Why would the rain go to waste? What about the fields that were watered? ("What fields, grandmother? It was you that the rain was looking for, it was us.")

When I started writing, I remembered the afentis' words and I tried to turn them into verses in the language in which grandmother narrated them to us.

> *However much it may rain,*
> *if we were to be afraid,*
> *if we were to be careful not to get wet,*
> *then what's the point of rain?*

"Original idea," a friend of mine told me.

"Ancestral," I replied.

"Ancestral?"

The most astonishing thing, which added a lot to the mystery (if it was a mystery) of Batistas, was his death. The previous evening, so the story goes, he gathered his children, grandchildren, great grandchildren and told them:

"Tomorrow I'm dying."

They were surprised.

"What are you talking about, afentis? Perish the thought!"

"Tomorrow I'm dying," Batistas repeated steadily. "I'm telling you so that you won't be scared."

He was chatting until late, giving instructions about the estate. And at the crack of dawn, he took a blanket, staggered out, put it on the ground, lay down just like for an afternoon nap on the hot days of August, and he died.

Everything that happened looked so unreal that the little children that gathered were ready to take hands and play ("Ring around the rosy…").

And something like that happened at the funeral. In front of the coffin, in front of the priests and the *hexapteryga*, the children walked in a row with their inevitably happy note. The funereal psalms were getting mixed up not knowing with what, and they were being altered, and the *hexapteryga* were becoming flags and kites.

The priests were protesting.

What kind of funeral was that? Why did they call them? The grandchildren and the great grandchildren might as well have performed the service.

And it was not just the day before that Batistas sensed his death. Two weeks earlier, he had called all his debtors to the estate, small land owners and hardworking people, lots of them. They came frightened and filled up the room.

Batistas brought a leather bag packed with promissory notes. He took them out one by one; he would put his hand in and take them out as if they were walnuts:

"Yiannis Nikola."

"Yes, my afentis."

"Can you pay in two weeks?"

"My afentis, you know…."

"Not much talking. Answer with a simple 'yes' or 'no.'"

"No, my afentis."

"Okay. I cannot wait. Take your note back!"

"Costis Kalathas."

"Yes, my afentis."

"Can you pay in two weeks?"

"No, my afentis."

"Okay, take your note back!"

"Demetris Podinas."

"Yes, my afentis."

"Can you pay in two weeks?"

"No, my afentis."

"Okay, take your note back!"

He thus returned all the promissory notes back to the astounded debtors.

"Now, go on your way, and next time, manage your accounts better!"

However, one of them replied affirmatively to Batistas' question.

"Can you pay in two weeks?"

"I can, my afentis."

Batistas was surprised.

"Can you in one week?"

"I can."

Batistas got irritated.

"Can you now?"

"I can, my afentis."

"Good, wait until the end to pay."

When everybody left, Batistas said to him:

"Okay, you paid. Take your note back."

"But I didn't pay, my afentis."

"You paid, I said! On your way now! Go!"

Everything was fine, but we expected something more from grandmother. We wanted her to tell us about a closed, haunted room, perhaps, where no one had ever entered.

She would laugh.

Tell us, grandmother, tell us, don't laugh. Can there be such a big estate without a haunted room, from where, at midnight, one could hear noises and voices and strange laughter and weeping?

Midnight has an effect on children, and it had an even greater effect in those days, when midnight was farther away, darker and more inaccessible, when it had not been exposed and degraded like today that people sing it and dance it and pass it by unnoticed and it has become "early" and it has become "what's the rush, it's only midnight."

We would dig into whatever grandmother was not telling us, we would dig into whatever she was not relating to us to find in her narrations what we could not find in father's. Because, even if he didn't know about afentis Batistas, even if he didn't know grand-mother's fairy tales and songs, he too had a lot to tell us on the winter nights. How he, still a little child, became an orphan and left for England when he was sixteen to work and send money to help support his three younger siblings. How, when he was barely eighteen, he enrolled as a volunteer in the British army and fought at Transvaal. He needed money badly, he said, and he was also influenced by the British propaganda. He would tell us about the Zulus, how the British would "mow them down" with their Mann-licher rifles while the Zulus had only bows and some old guns whose bullets could not even reach the lines of the British. He would tell us about the terrified women who would fix their eyes wide open and were looking without saying a word and about the black little children who were crying constantly. And he would tell us also about his sergeant, a nervy, whimsical brutal Londoner, who could not stand screaming and crying and he would kick the children fiercely with his army boots and make them bleed.

He was kicking them with his army boots? We would get more upset about that than about the "mowing down" of the Zulus, perhaps because we had "cognitive images."

"Didn't you lift your hand, father, to hit him?"

Even though my father would laugh, we kept it inside us, and, when he told us one day about the British battalion that the Zulus had ambushed on the side of a hill and massacred, we asked with impatient hope:

22

"Was the sergeant too in the battalion?"

Unfortunately, father could not satisfy us.

"What a question! If the sergeant had been there, I would have been there too."

It would be too much for me to believe that our childlike soul wished in a naïve secret little corner for father to die too rather than let the sergeant get away. However, strange feelings tormented me many years later when I found myself for a few days with a group of reporters in South Africa. They took us to a Zulu village, a few miles from Pretoria. And then I saw the same half-naked terrified women with knotty knees being whipped by our South African tour guides, because they would not come out of their huts to be photographed with us.

"They are wily," they told us. "They don't come out so that you will go in and we won't be able see if you give them a tip."

And I saw the same black little children crying and looking at us persistently with their bright little eyes, like the Morning Star, while they were watching their mothers being whipped and, since they were holding on to their mothers' clothes, getting also a small share of the whipping. The way they were looking at us showed that they suspected it was our fault. As far as I am concerned, if they only knew about my father too!

I did not lift my hand either, of course, to hit the tour guides, and I could already see my father constantly following me with the Mannlicher step by step, and suddenly I could see me becoming one with him, and suddenly I could see me too holding a Mannlicher. I could hear his narrations again, and I would join in and narrate too. Then, just as suddenly, I would come back to reality and feel distressed.

"Is it these children that you had come to kill, father, is it these little eyes that you had come to close? Didn't you consider that God would not be able to see without these little eyes? Much as I know how badly you needed money, what becomes of me now, father? Didn't you at least consider that maybe a son of yours would be writing verses, and how would he escape, how would he keep quiet? Do you know that the children were uninformed, that they were completely uninformed, and that one of them smiled at me? He smiled at me, father, do you understand? He smiled at me a knife stab."

I was thus opening a painful subject, I was opening a wound for an unimaginably beloved father, dead for years. And I was trying to reinforce his excuses. I was arguing that perhaps, even subconsciously, the hatred that he had his whole life for the British, and which he instilled at home, had its roots in the deception of their propaganda, which carried him away to Transvaal, to the kicks of the sergeant from London.

Under the whips, the women were forced to come out of their huts, running like sheep, and the reporters were insatiably photographed with them.

Definitely something else must have existed in grandmother's narrations, which father could sense.

"You took away our customers, old gal."

"You know better, son. I guess children prefer grandmother and grandfather to be telling them stories and fairy tales. It suits us better."

With this realization, grandmother was unintentionally touching an interesting subject. Namely, that perhaps the fact that grandfathers and grandmothers come from a more distant world, from another, as far as the children are concerned, world, is important. And indeed, remember how differently we used to look at them. In the case of our own grandmother, in fact, her world was made a more "different world," more distant, by the mezzanine, by the six steps that we would go up, the six steps that we would swim (plaf, plaf, plaf) in order to find her. Besides, perhaps we could sense that father still had a long time ahead of him to tell us his stories while grandmother might leave any day. And she was our only representative of the other world. Neither did we have another grandmother, nor a grandfather. She was our only grandmother with the same meaning and the same tone and the same tenderness that we say "an only son" and "an only daughter" and that the church calls (redundantly) Jesus "the only begotten son." "An only grandmother" (beautiful word, make a note of it), an only grandmother, who had no greater joy, who had no other contribution, than to tell us stories. And even father's thunderous voice "of today" could not compete with grandmother's quiet, frail, soft, wrinkled, "past" sweet little voice.

Therefore, her stories had a different fascination, even compared to father's most adventurous narrations, such as the narrations from the time when he was a forester. They might, he said, notify him suddenly about a fire, and he had to start immediately on his horse to go from Nicosia to Troodos, for there were then no cars, no carriages, nor roads to the mountains. He would pass, sometimes at night, through a thick forest where the Hasamboulia, three legendary "fugitives," had their den. They often jumped in front of him asking for cigarettes and cognac, which he would anticipate and always have in his saddle bag. They were good to him. They would joke:

"Switch to a different brand sometimes, afentis, don't be stingy. We are fed up with these cotton cigarettes."

"I'm not stingy, my friends. Just tell me what you like."

However much we did not like father's dealings with the Hasamboulia, even though we understood his position, we would not discuss them. In our minds the forest had the prominent place, not the "fugitives," the forest, which we had heard about in fairy tales and which we had never seen. A dark black forest which came alive at night and roared and spread thousands of arms to enfold you and which hid ghosts and spirits that made the little animals and the birds perch frightened and quiet. The "fugitives" were nothing more than an added branch.

In such a forest (here grandmother intervenes and pushes father to the side) had a prince been lost one morning, but fortunately the good fairy happened to be passing by and helped him get to a clearing before it got dark.

"How can I repay you?" asked the prince.

"You will find a way," replied the good fairy.

And it was at that clearing that he found the poor little cottage and asked Anthi for water. The girl ran and brought him a glass that was sparkling clean. The thirsty prince grabbed it but, as he was bringing it to his lips, he saw a piece of hay floating. That's strange. He frowned. He looked at Anthi. Should he tell her or just keep quiet? He remained hesitant. He remembered the words of the good fairy. Who knows, maybe the beautiful girl was the good fairy herself and was testing him. No, he would not say anything. And he started drinking slowly so that he would not swallow the hay, which kept sticking to his lips forcing him to take breaks.

Time passed and the prince was dying of curiosity. He was thinking:

"She must have seen the hay when I returned to her the empty glass. How come she didn't say anything? Was she really the good fairy?"

When he fell in love with her and took her to the palace to make her his wife, he asked her:

"So, tell me, are you the good fairy?"

Anthi was surprised:

"What good fairy? I don't understand."

The prince could not keep it any longer.

"What was the hay in the glass?"

Anthi pretended to be surprised:

"Hay? There was hay in the glass?"

The prince suspects other things and speaks harshly:

"Was it magic to seduce me?"

Anthi got scared with the suspicion, she became pale, her eyes filled with tears.

"That's what you think of me, my master?"

And here grandmother's song pops in with lyricism and a humorous tone:

Magic to the one I love, magic to the one I'd die for?
I'd rather stay unmarried a thousand years and even more.

She is forced to confess that she put the hay in the glass so that he would drink the cold water slowly lest he should get sick since he was so sweaty and tired.

Happy and free from the affliction of suspicion, the prince replies, trying to justify himself:

If not for the hay, "you enchanted me" I wouldn't say
and you wouldn't admit you love me
keeping your stubbornness at bay.

"Weren't you afraid of the forest, father?" we would ask with admiration. "Weren't you afraid of ghosts?"

He did not believe in ghosts and spirits, he said. Only once….
He stops.

We prick up our ears. We did not know anything about the spirits of the forests and the ravines, the wild ones, so to speak, however much we knew about the goblins of the houses, the domesticated ones, so to speak, however many details we knew about them. We knew, for instance, that during the Twelve Days, if you leave the closet door open, the mother goblin goes in and gives birth to baby goblins, which never leave the house in all eternity; they are "local" and not even the priest with his holy water has the right to chase them away, and the house is doomed unless maybe there is an earthquake and they get scared and scatter away. (The story goes that they call them from the depths of the Earth: "Come! The houses of the people will fall! Quickly! The houses of the people will fall!")

"Well?"

"Nothing."

"What nothing?" (You too, father? Just like grandmother? Tell us!)

27

One day he was scared, he said.

We huddle together. Here come the ghosts, here come, no doubt, the ghosts of the forest.

"Well?"

He is trying to change the subject; we don't let him (He shouldn't have started). We pull him by the sleeve.

"Well?"

"Do you want to hear?"

What does it mean, do we want to hear? Of course we want to hear!

He hesitates. Don't look the other way! We take his face with both hands, we turn it to confront us eye to eye, we immobilize it:

There! Don't you understand that you are competing with grandmother?

We stamp our feet impatiently.

"Well?"

He cannot escape.

It was past midnight, he says, pitched dark. On his way to the forest of Kykkos, which had caught fire, he had to pass by a place where a few days earlier they had found a young forester killed and half eaten by the vultures. From the moment he left, the idea that he would see the forester in front of him was fixed burning in his mind:

"You see what they did to me, boss? At least, is anyone looking after my wife and my children, boss?"

All the way he could think of nothing else. His mind was stuck on the forester. And the closer he got, the more fear was gnawing at him.

"You see what your friends to whom you give cigarettes and cognac did to me, boss?"

"No, it can't be the Hasamboulia," my father would protest.

"Then who? Then who?" (And like an echo: Then who? Then who?)

"I don't know, I don't know."

Suddenly, when he reached the murder scene, he saw something like cotton, something like white flakes unfolding and running in front of the horse's legs. He caught his breath. There, it's time for the forester to jump out too.

("At least, is anyone looking after my wife and my children, boss?")

The strange thing is that the horse was galloping quietly with his ears undisturbed. He bends down and whispers to him so that the white flakes won't hear:

"Don't you see anything?"

The horse was calm just like before. He took courage.

If the horse can't see them, they don't exist, he thought. Horses cannot be deceived. He tapped him lightly on the neck with his hand. The horse speeded up his gallop and took the mountain slope.

"So the forester's ghost didn't come out?"

"How would it come out since horses don't get ideas in their heads?"

Ideas? So everything is ideas? Grandmother has beaten you, father!

Today I know that, if father wanted, he could tell us about the fairies of his village, Lapithos, and fascinate us, because a few years later I was reading an occult book that claimed that the fairies of the island lived in Lapithos at the "Kefalovryso" and in the lemon groves. It gave a description of them, it said that many people had seen them, and it mentioned old and new dates and names:

"On April 24, 1938, while Yiannis Karaviotis was going at the crack of dawn to water his orchard, at the bridge of Vathirkakas, he saw about ten half-naked girls with long flowing hair sitting in a row with their legs dangling in the river, talking and laughing loudly, just like the girls from Nicosia who spent the summer at the village, as if they imitated them, as if they were enacting and putting up a show to make fun of them. Two or three even had male roles. Yiannis watched for a while, but suddenly he understood, got scared, and let out a scream. The girls immediately disappeared in the oleanders, and Yiannis became mute, and it took him three months to be able to speak again."

About the white flakes we just asked without any interest:

"Did you at least ('at least'!) find out who killed the forester?"

Yes, they did. Mavros.

Mavros was a ruthless Turkish robber, who had his den in the Paphos area. Even though he sometimes made his appearance farther down and ambushed carriages and ox-carts going slowly and with difficulty up the slope of Kakoratzia, some twenty miles from Nicosia, he did not dare get into Troodos, where the Hasamboulia had their dens. So he must have had a reason to risk coming down to kill the forester.

"He did it because of us," said the Hasamboulia to father, "to get us in trouble. Just wait and one day we'll drop by and wipe him out."

My father talked to us about Mavros with great hatred. And he would tell us with uncontrollable satisfaction and joy that the Hasamboulia did not have to "drop by and wipe him out" because a young shepherd boy "wiped him out" in the meantime.

Mavros, so the story goes, had gone one morning at dawn to steal a sheep from a sheepfold. He went in like the man of the house with the audacity that everybody's fear of him gave him. It seems that many times in the past he had taken sheep from the same sheepfold, but the shepherd never dared stop him. It was his bad luck, however, that this time Koutsogiorgos, the shepherd, was away in the village and had left the sheepfold to the care of his son, a boy barely fifteen years old. The shepherd boy heard the noise, he saw Mavros take the sheep, and he jumped up with the rifle.

"Hey! Put the sheep down!" he shouted at him.

Mavros turned around slowly and looked scornfully at the audacious boy. He was not used to such reception.

"*Sus, be oğlan!*" he answered angrily. "Where is your father?"

"Leave my father out of this. I'm here now."

"Okay, tell your father that Mavros took a sheep and that he can debit my account."

And he laughed loudly.

At hearing his name, the shepherd boy flinched for a moment. Mavros! The same Mavros whom the whole world feared? Even though for sure his father would not be angry if he gave in, it so happened that it was his first time holding a rifle and he was squeezing it in his arms and the rifle was squeezing his hand back! No, it cannot be done.

"I don't know about your accounts. Put the sheep down!"

Mavros replied with a heavy Turkish insult.

"*Siktir, deyus* boy!"

And he started to go. The shepherd boy did not reply. The rifle wriggled in his hand ("Now!"). He aimed and fired. It was the first time in his life that he was firing. Mavros was hit on the leg and he knelt. He did not expect it.

"*Be pezevenk, orospu tohumu* (something like that!)," he shouted with pain and tried to get his gun down from his shoulder. He didn't have time. The shepherd boy fired again, and Mavros fell.

They heard the shots in the village and ran worried.

"They came from Koutsogiorgos' sheepfold."

Koutsoyiorgos was running first and behind him his wife frantic. He was turning and in vain shouting at her every little while to stay back. The mother would not hear of it.

"You left the child alone? What were you thinking? Holy Mary, help us."

When they arrived breathless, they could not believe their eyes. Mavros was lying down dead and, farther down, the shepherd boy was sitting on a rock guarding him with the rifle ready.

"Mavros!"

"He came to steal and I killed him!" the boy said simply.

The area and the whole island were relieved by Mavros' death, the shepherd boy was made a hero, the British Governor expressed his "satisfaction."

Contrary to Mavros, the Hasamboulia were in good terms with the people, who slowly got connected with them and were helping and hiding them. They even admired them. In a time without heroism on the island, an island which preserved very much alive the medieval heroic songs of Dighenis Akritas, the lost heroism, which was swelling in their chests and was bringing tears to their eyes, was grabbed, especially for the simple village people, by the three fugitives and by the fact that they always managed to remain uncaught and to move under the noses of the policemen who, after all, were policemen of the new foreign tyrant and had British leaders, who were becoming a laughing stock. A little while longer and even the Hasamboulia might find a place in the folk songs and in the verses of the poets with their nomadic poetry which traveled to the four corners of the island, to the festivals of Apostolos Andreas and of Kataklysmos, of the Olive and of Kykkos, of Ayios Georgios Kontos and of Ayios Mamas, of Ayios Panteleimon and of the Acheropiitos and of Archangelos; the nomadic poetry of the festivals, which, having started deep in the centuries, was searching for fascinating heroic or dramatic themes of poverty and love and courage and human fate. A little while longer and the elderly women storytellers might confuse the Hasamboulia and add them somewhere, interpose them somewhere. And the fact that the three bold and aggressive fugitives were brothers made them even more likeable and gave a different dimension to the theme.

Within the frame of this certain restrained and secret admiration for the Hasamboulia, which was afraid to be expressed, belongs, it seems, the fact that my father named his beloved horse Hasamboulis. Well, he was telling us that once in his report of expenses, instead of putting down so many okas of barley for the horse, by mistake he wrote down so many okas of barley for Hasamboulis. The British accountant was surprised:

"Do we provide Hasamboulis with barley?"

One day the Hasamboulia found out that my father called his horse Hasamboulis, and they were not sure that he didn't do it just to mock them. Someone may have also dropped a hint. They asked him.

"From admiration for your courage," said my father.

And of course he meant it.

"Do your bosses the British know about this?"

"What do the British understand about such things?" he answered.

And he told them about the episode with the accountant:

"Are we obligated to provide Hasamboulis with barley?"

Father's admiration for the three fugitives may have had something to do also with the fact that the first (and, for a long time, the only) family book that we had at home when we were children was "Delis the robber and Angelo, the priest's daughter." It was a massive book—I don't know who the author was, because I was not interested then in the author nor did I know whether books were written by authors. For children a book is there just as a table is there, just as a closet is there. Do we know who made the table, do we know who made the closet? Do we ask?

The book described the adventures of a robber, Delis, and his love for Angelo, the priest's beautiful daughter. Father was reading it every night in the light of a paraffin lamp, or better, he was reviewing it for he must have read it many times. And for many times we had to stay and listen to him narrating it to us and showing us the pictures. So many times that without being able to read, as soon as you showed us a picture, we could tell you the caption right away: "Tell them not to speak rudely to Angelo, because I'll get down to the village one night, and alas for them."

Up until the middle of the book, father was an admirer of Delis. And we with him. From then on, when Delis was starting to become bloodthirsty, he would turn against him. And we with him. And father would be okay if during the next reading (the next review) he were not initially an admirer of Delis. Knowing what would follow, we would get confused and we would comment:

"Are you forgetting that later on he will become a murderer, father?"

"The book hasn't said that yet," he would reply.

"It said it another time."

"It doesn't matter. Today we don't know anything."

And at the end of the book was father's favorite caption when Delis had already lost all of father's respect and had fallen under relentless disfavor: "I've hardly ever been scared of anyone and I'll be scared of you?" someone was saying to the robber.

Father had tears in his eyes while he was reading it (while he was reciting it) as if he himself were the one defying Delis. "I've hardly ever...." And he would add:

"And he was not even armed!"

At the time, we understood completely father's admiration. Therefore, I found it strange when, while looking for information for my story, I heard old people from Lapithos telling me about an ancestor of father's, Miltaros, strong and brave like no other in the area. He could fight against the whole village. He had a tail, do you understand?

Yes, yes, a tail. Many people saw it, and even his mother was revealing it to her close friends:

"I'm afraid that it may be Satan that stuck his tail."

They would comfort her.

"Don't say that. God has a tail too, God sticks His tail too sometimes. He is for something big, I'm telling you. Be happy about it, don't be sad."

And there were other things too besides the tail. He was born with three teeth. The women in the neighborhood would go and see him. They had heard about children being born with one tooth, but with three teeth, they had never heard of anyone.

And the stories began too: The night that his mother was in labor, they said, the dogs in the neighborhood kept barking strangely with the ominous dragging cry that forebodes the death of the man of the house ("He will destroy his master. Kill him or give him away").

He could uproot trees with one hand, they said. First he would ask to be beaten until his breasts would swell and become as red as chili peppers and he would feel his tail move. Then he would grab the trees one by one and pull them out like corn ears. Wild medlar trees, no joke.

Nevertheless, one day he said:

"Mother, I'm leaving. I may cause great damage here, great harm. I was destined for elsewhere. There was a mistake. The other day my father said something to me, and I saw him as a wild medlar tree. I have to prevent it."

And he left. Once there was a rumor that he was in Abessynia, in the emperor's bodyguard corps, and that he made a lot of money, which disappeared after his death and nobody knew what happened to it.

And they told a strange story about his death; that, supposedly, one day someone saw his tail and spread the story in the jungle. The tribe was upset. They decided that he was a sorcerer. They devised a plan and went one night to his house and slaughtered him while he was asleep. The house, they said, was shaken from his bellowing. He was writhing and thrashing for half an hour. They stripped him naked, cut his tail off, and burned it with magic spells and dances.

I said that I was surprised when I first heard the story of Miltaros. It was strange that father had hidden it from us while he was moved to tears by that "I've hardly ever been scared."

"He never told you anything?"

"Never. He was reading to us about Delis!"

And I was even more surprised when a cousin of mine in Athens told me one day about someone at work who had provoked him:

"Don't worry, I'll show him the meaning of Miltaros' fist!"

So he knew? Who had told him? Seeing him so brawny and strong, though, I realized with bitterness that there was some meaning in his being told about Miltaros. But how could they tell us since I, the half-portioned one, would hear too?

Anyway, that was the second thing that father had hidden from us. And, no doubt, if he were alive and I asked him why, he would give me his usual answer when he wanted to evade:

"Put on the stole and hear my confession, Koronaios!"

As they told us, Koronaios was someone very curious, who became so annoying with his questions that, as soon as he entered the coffeehouse, one by one all the patrons would get up and leave.

The name of Koronaios came down to us just like the name of Ropas. "You owe to Ropas" meant "You are crazy." Now, why all those who owed to Ropas were crazy I don't know. The fact is that even the teachers used the phrase at school to scold a naughty student.

"What happened to you? Do you owe to Ropas?"

"Who was Ropas?" I would ask.

"Some doctor."

"Crazy?"

"No."

"Then what?"

"I don't know, Koronaios!"

I would not have minded that father called me "Koronaios" sometimes if my brothers and sisters had not heard and stuck the nickname to me.

"Quiet, Koronaios!"

I was afraid to ask however much I was dying of curiosity. I would complain to mother:

"They called me Koronaios."

She would laugh.

"You can be asking me; don't worry about the others."

Even in fairy tales when grandmother would talk about a golden "corona," they would turn and look at me and laugh. Grandmother found out about it and would use the word "crown" instead. Crown? They did not spare her.

"What's a crown, grandmother?"

"Corooona," they themselves would reply.

I went through a lot to get rid of the slander. And fortunately, it was confined within the family and did not spread in the neighborhood and the school, otherwise I would be ruined.

Get rid of it? Many years later, one day, out of the blue, my oldest sister, Irinia, said to me:

"You are asking too many questions, Koronaios."

And I wonder now why I had so much curiosity as a child. What was the use of the questions, what was the use of the causes and the caused? Better not to have asked anything, better not to have found out anything. It served me right to be ridiculed like that.

Father's comment "And he was not even armed" was similar to the comments of an old man from Asia Minor, owner of a wandering open-air, and of course silent, movie theater. He would stand behind the small projector and explain:

"As you can see, the doctor and the girl hit it off."

And then, when the projection would suddenly be interrupted:

"Remain seated, it's nothing. Just a small screw, and the doctor will find his girl again."

"Hurry up, he may leave!" someone from the audience would reply.

When I started putting down on paper elements and ideas about my narration, I had forgotten the exact phrasing of the caption and I attempted to go and ask Irinia, the only one who had remained from the beehive of the house. She was old and sick in bed with a hazy mind.

She looked at me sweetly as if thanking me for bringing back the memories, and looking as if in a daze. From her extinguished eyes passed a glint. She smiled and whispered:

"I've hardly ever been scared of anyone and I'll be scared of you?"

She did not call me "Koronaios" even though it may have been in her smile, it may have been one of its ingredients. And I would give anything to have answered her:

"Yes, look now what has become of Koronaios! All those questions for nothing!"

In our illnesses "Delis the robber and Angelo, the priest's daughter" was on our bed so that we could leaf through it and it could keep us company and we could feel its weight on our feet at night and it could hold down the quilt in the winter like an anchor. We would look for it in the morning when our eyes would open a little through the fever of measles.

"Mama, pass me Delis."

How I remember my own measles. Half of the children in kindergarten had been swept away. I would hear the mother of our little neighbor cry and shout and I would ask unsuspecting:

"What's wrong with Yiannakis' mother?"

"Who knows!"

It was not until my sisters grew up and love played in their eyes and feeling opened its windows to more varied emotions that other extracurricular books appeared in our house, "The Two Orphans," "Notre Dame," "Kassiani," "Genovefa," "Les Miserables," to replace "Delis the robber and Angelo, the priest's daughter," which seems to have been lost during a move, because I was looking for it and could not find it anywhere. Father was now completely absorbed in "Les Miserables."

Later on, as a university student in Athens, I looked in vain in the old-books bookstores for a copy of the unforgettable book to put it on the floor like then with my brothers and sisters and leaf through its pictures, find father's beloved caption which brought tears to his eyes. "I've hardly ever been scared of anyone and I'll be scared of you?"

I needed that caption from another respect too, the way I was entering life with so much drama behind me and so much fear.

Father used to tell us about his horse's jealousy when he got married. The horse neighed menacingly whenever he saw my mother, and he would not let her feed him or brush him.

"He won't eat from my hand," she would complain.

"Leave it there for him, and when he gets hungry, he will be only too happy to eat it, you'll see."

But the horse would neither eat nor be happy. The hay just stayed there unwanted and untouched.

In vain did my father talk to him, in vain did he try to make him understand, in vain was he forced to scold him and give him a little slap.

"Hey, it was for her that we used to travel so many miles to Famagusta. Don't you remember? Don't you remember the apprentice girls, the flowers they would throw us?"

And then again:

"Her mother softened up; you are the problem now? What an unyielding nuisance you are, anyway."

The horse was stubborn, uncompromising. Father was afraid and he double locked the door of the stable whenever he was away. Until one day he forgot to secure the bolt and the horse came out threatening. Mother, who was pregnant with her first child, heard the noise in the yard and ran scared and locked herself in the kitchen. Hasamboulis saw her and besieged her and started kicking the door fiercely and furiously. With her screams, the neighborhood gathered, and two or three men who were passing by got in too. They tried to frighten the horse and move him away.

"Away from there! Back to your stall!"

The horse was infuriated even more by the foreign intervention and stood high up on two legs.

And then they were forced to beat him with broom-sticks and stakes and canes. They beat him up badly. Blood was dripping from his face and neck. He was all sweaty and breathing heavily. Shortly, he gave in and let them lead him back to the stable.

When father returned, he found mother in bed very pale and exhausted. She told him crying what had happened, the neighbors told him even more and in their own way:

"Your horse is a murderer. Make sure you get rid of him before some disaster strikes. You should have seen how he behaved! Your poor wife was scared to death. God have mercy on her, and not let her lose the baby. He was biting the sticks like a rabid animal."

"What sticks?"

"Well, how were the people going to restrain him, with caresses? It's a good thing that they ran to help."

"They beat him?"

The neighbor got angry:

"You should be thanking God that your wife is safe, pal. What more do you want?"

My father ignored the comment. Something else was flashing in his eyes.

"Who beat him?"

The neighbors got scared.

"Passers-by, we don't know them, we asked them for help since we couldn't manage alone."

They turned and hurried out.

"The man is completely insane. That was his thank you. Instead of worrying that his wife may lose the child…."

Father hugged mother; he caressed her tenderly.

"It was my fault."

He took his service pistol and went to the stable. Mother's voice reached behind him.

"He's a horse, he doesn't know. Don't harm him."

"He doesn't know? That's what you think."

He approached Hasamboulis. The blood had dried on his face and neck, his eye was black and swollen. Father stuck his face to his muzzle.

"What did you do, you little rascal?"

His voice sounded heavy and hoarse.

"I'll kill you."

Hasamboulis pouted for a moment even if he wasn't scared, even if he knew that his master could not harm him.

"What got into you? My wife is one thing, you are another."

The horse rubbed caressingly his head on his shoulder.

Father was getting angry and at the same time he was looking furtively at Hasamboulis' wounds. Angrily, he groped them lightly (My hand was just passing by, just happened to be passing by).

Your hand was passing by? The horse understood and neighed ("I knew it").

"Stop that, you piece of crap."

Mother's screams could be heard from inside:

"Don't harm him."

Slowly my father softened up. He just had to salvage something from his anger. So he tended very harshly to Hasamboulis' wounds. He was pushing him:

"Turn this way! Turn that way!"

He was almost slapping him with the cold water. And he sealed the incident with a threat:

"If we lose the child, you and I will have a little chat."

Fortunately, they didn't lose the child, and they didn't have a little chat.

Nevertheless, Hasamboulis could not stay at the house. The women in the neighborhood would also incite my mother:

"He's a murderer, my kyra-Kalomoira. He will do the same again, you'll see."

"I am scared, I can't," she kept telling my father.

And father had no choice. He started looking for a buyer, someone who would take good care of Hasamboulis and love him even if he didn't pay well. And finally he found someone.

"Don't worry. He won't even know he changed masters," he assured him. "You know me."

He caressed him, he kissed him, and he gave him over. He gave him over, and the house was empty behind him. Mother would see him sad, and it was breaking her heart.

"Don't worry about me," he was telling her. "I'll get another horse and I'll get over it. You just take care of the child."

But neither was he getting another horse nor was he getting over it. Whenever he had time he would drop by to see Hasamboulis. He was talking about him like an old friend.

"I'll go for a walk to see Hasamboulis and then I'll go to the coffeehouse for a while. I won't be long."

Mother was very understanding. In order to please him, she would ask:

"How is he? Has he adjusted?"

"He's not eating well, he got a little thinner. I shouldn't be going so often to see him, because he got spoiled and now he waits for me to feed him. I'll go less often, don't worry. You just watch the child."

He didn't go less often. One day, in fact, he came home riding on Hasamboulis. It was a triumphant return, something like an entrance to a captured city.

The neighborhood was staring astonished.

"What's this now? It can't be; he's crazy."

Upon entering the house father said:

"I've brought him back. He promised not to do it again."

Mother smiled with understanding. She realized that there was no more room for disagreement.

The horse neighed loudly when he saw his old stall and stamped his feet noisily on the pavement.

The neighborhood completed its criticism:

"That ungodly one! He brought back Hasamboulis! I just can't believe it."

"Ridiculous and outrageous. Not thinking of his wife!"

Guessing the comments and the gossips, father went to the front door, saw two or three women there, two or three in the street and on the balconies, and he shouted at them:

"Yes, I've brought him back. The Hasamboulia got angry and they said they'll come down and alas for us. Just like Delis. Have you heard of him?"

The women did not reply. They scattered and left the balconies and closed the windows.

"What Delis was he talking about? He is totally insane. He doesn't deserve such a wife, fresh like cool water."

"Cursed poverty."

The only thing that grandmother never mentioned to us—and we would not ask about either—was how she found herself at the estate of afentis Batistas; which grandfather, which grandmother, which parents interceded, whether they were alive at the time or whether they had died, whether they lived at the estate or not. And it seems that we would not ask, either because we were not interested or because the other things occupied and absorbed us.

The other things absorbed us? Our subconscious was not absorbed by the narrations (the subconscious has a special destination and is disconnected from the goals and interests of the conscious) and was keeping in a drawer its pending questions. So one day Yiorgos opened the drawer:

"What about you, grandmother? Did they bring you down in a basket?"

It is a good thing that he asked. The mistake was that with the phrase that he used—characteristic of grandmother's narrations—we all laughed and grandmother with us and she did not answer.

Incidentally, I have to say here that when you are four years old and they tell you that "they brought someone down in a basket," you imagine a real basket with a rope up to heaven that God is holding and unraveling carefully and watching out for rough spots until the basket gently touches the ground and touches exactly where He intended it.

And I was then—I've said that already—four years old. A long time passed before I understood the meaning of the heavenly basket, before I understood its drama when I would see thousands of baskets coming down, and I was not sure that it was God who was unraveling their ropes and that He was watching out for rough spots and that He intended them.

Anyway, it was obvious from grandmother's narrations that at the estate there lived many branches of the Batistas family, and among them was grandmother with her younger sister, Katelia. And it was the branches that, after the afentis' death, dissolved and sold the estate very cheaply and threw grandmother into the poverty that I have mentioned.

"Don't you have a picture of him?" we would ask.

How could she? There were no photographers except for a German in Skala, many miles away.

We had an insatiable curiosity about the afentis, a curiosity that would not accept the stories about him to run out, and had its mouth open so that you could throw in endlessly and still not fill it up.

"Tell us more, grandmother."

And we would gather closer.

"Why is your brain working so much?" grandmother wondered.

It was working, indeed. We drew afentis Batistas again and again and we wrote down his name in the kindergarten and elementary school notebooks next to the Greek flags and the first caricatures of houses and trees: "The afentis and Katingo," "The afentis and the intellectual," "The afentis and his cats," "The death of the afentis."

And we had to explain to our classmates and the teachers who were asking.

"It's afentis Batistas."

"Who is afentis Batistas?"

"Our ancestor."

We concentrated one-sidedly on afentis Batistas and would forget about father's poor descent.

For my part, I continued to mold him again and again through high school when grandmother had already been dead for years. It was a kind of obsession, especially when my first verses started shyly dropping hints and preparing their bridgehead (even though the afentis was not at all for youthful verses).

I remember that, at the first step of adolescence, after my mother's death, I was filled with extreme sadness, which worried my father even though it was justified since four years earlier I had lost both of my brothers. He was worried also because I happened to be so frail, skin-and-bones, a suckling, a "late-seed" as they called me without being afraid that I might ask what the word meant anyway.

(Late-seed? I might not have been a late-seed at all if my mother had not believed that, as long as she was still breastfeeding, she would not get pregnant with another child.

"Six is enough," she would say.

It seems that at the time other methods of birth control were unknown on the island, and I was being used as "the pill." For five years, I was "the pill." And by then I enjoyed it so much that I pulled my mother by her dress secretly and persistently whenever we had guests at home.

"Let's go inside so that I can suckle. I'm shy here."

The excuse was pointless, because, even if I were not shy, my mother would definitely be ["Let's go inside so that I can suckle. We are shy here!"].

She pretended that she was asking:

"What do you want, baby?"

And she would take me inside before I had time to answer.

In what way this unnaturally prolonged breastfeeding has helped me or harmed me physically and emotionally I don't know; what dependence, what identification or even what childishness it has cultivated in me.

As for the methods of birth control, they remained unknown to the large majority of the people until much later; so much so that people tell the following joke:

A British tourist woman ran into two shepherd boys with their flocks near the ruins of the temple of Aphrodite at Kouklia in Paphos. She approached them and told them in broken Greek:

"I want to know love at the ruins just like in the old days. Can you help me, please?"

"We'll help you, madam," the shepherd boys answered without knowing what she meant, and they followed her to the ruins, where they finally realized what the British woman wanted.

"Since I don't want to have a child," she said, "I will put a small thing on you. Okay?"

They did not object.

"Since she doesn't want to have a child, that's okay."

The continuation two days later at the village coffeehouse:

"Listen, Hambis, do you care if the British woman has a child or not?"

"Let her have a child for all I care."

"Then, shall we go and take off the stupid things she put on us?")

"My God, all I have now is a leftover, a tiny branch," my father would say, "help it grow strong."

I had to "grow strong" because whether the name of my family would survive or be extinguished hung on me (Fortunately, I had no sense of my responsibility then).

"It's as if I were stealing from the churches," my father would complain.

He would take me out with him and hold me by the hand and squeeze it as if he were afraid that I too might leave him. We were a tragic couple that it hurts me to talk about, and until now I persistently avoided making it a subject of mine, as if it were something that I should not mention in case my father did not want me to, in case he was not supposed to find out that I knew.

(I don't know how preoccupied we are by the tragic couples that we meet on a walk, on a deserted bench, in the bus, in church, silent and unparticipating in the world, in the sun, in the rain: the father and the "retarded" child, a young man sixteen or eighteen years old, walking hand in hand; the couple whose only two boys have been "missing" for five years; the grandfather and the grandmother who go to the play area of the Municipal Gardens, where they used to take their little Armonia, to see again the white pony she used to sit on, to see again the swing she used to swing on; the mother who goes around in the streets in a skirt down to her ankles like her "spastic" daughter; the other mother in church who stands with her simpleton son at the men's pews).

He always tried to anticipate my wishes, ready to take me to the park, to the movies, to the Hungarian circus, to the football matches. I, for my part, never asked for anything that was outside the frame of our great calamity. I pretended that I liked this and that, even his reading to me the newspaper—the "Voice of Cyprus"—and even the main articles with the archaic "thee" and "thou."

He would climb up and strive to take hold of my hope, strive to hold on to my hope even though I was just a "leftover" and a "tiny branch." There are other things that count, there are counterbalances. He realized that I was not a "hardly ever scared of anyone" whom he admired, he realized that he could not present me as a "hardly ever scared of anyone" and he would comment in English to his friends so that I would not understand and put on airs:

"He is very clever!"

He didn't know that I was not even (not at least) clever. And fortunately when the truth was proven and the certificate came out final and unambiguous, my father was not alive.

Worried, he took me to a doctor. He was an old man, a refugee from Mersina. He examined me carefully and did not find anything physically wrong.

"You have something inside you that is tormenting you," he told me.

I did not answer.

"Besides all the other things, of course," he continued.

I realized that he was calling simply "other things" my mother and my brothers, trying to bypass our family tragedy.

"I don't know."

"Search for it."

I thought, I hesitated and finally I said it:

"Maybe it's afentis Batistas."

Yes, everything was tormenting me, both "the other things" and afentis Batistas, who kept surfacing intertwined with the happy old years when mother and brothers and grandmother were still alive, perhaps even, it was only the happy old years, and afentis Batistas may have been just an easy and convincing cover-up and pretense.

The doctor was surprised.

"Who?"

"The ancestor."

He bulged his eyes.

"What ancestor?"

I went out without answering, and the doctor called in my father.

"The child has a fear," said a neighbor. "Take him to kyra-Yiasemi, the midwife in Korvos, to rid him of it."

They notified kyra-Yiasemi. She asked us to wait until the moon was full. The moon became full and they took me to her. Kyra-Yiasemi brought a big plate with water which she had put outside the night before to catch the reflection of the moon, and which she had "read" with the magic charm of fear.

"Look at your face in the water and tell me how you see it," she said.

I looked at it. It was a little wrinkled and one eye seemed somewhat bigger than the other.

"The right one?"

"The left one."

"The left one? Let me see."

She agitated the water with her hand and scattered it "to the four winds" starting from the left.

"Okay," she said.

She took some bullet slugs and, after "reading" them with a mumbled unintelligible magic charm, she put them in a small pan on the hearth. When the slugs melted, she poured the molten lead in cold water so that whatever caused my fear would form and disappear.

The strange thing was that she was having a hard time figuring out what had formed, and she was looking at it from all sides.

As for me, I liked the mystic procedure, which reminded me of grandmother's fairy tales, and I ate with great appetite the roast they prepared for us at "Vrysi."

If I knew that kyra-Yiasemi was still alive, I would go and find her in Korvos and tell her that the image that had formed with the molten lead was a hounded stray dog that the slaughterer in Morphou chased and shot at, but missed and the dog got into my sister's house and sought refuge ("It doesn't have to be inside the house, even in the yard it's fine"), and he stayed in the yard for many years without daring to get out in the street, with the tail always tucked between his legs, without daring even once to wag it, even just to pretend a drop of joy, even just to show a drop of gratitude, like all the dogs of the world, just as all the dogs of the world have the irrefutable right to, without daring to bark even once, and he would run and hide terrified whenever he heard other people in the house besides us (Needless to say that it was a mistake to exclude us).

Another time the women in the neighborhood said that I was suffering from jaundice. After my mother's death, they considered it their obligation to interfere and give advice and indeed so much so that their husbands didn't like it.

"Where were you at this hour?"

"At the orphans' house, where else would I be?"

"Don't forget that the orphans have a father too, a widower."

"You should be ashamed of yourself!"

The jaundice could be cured either by a priest or two or three others who knew the magic charm. My father did not choose the priest, and he took me to an old man in Avlakia, the infamous neighborhood of Skala. The old man took a red string, cut it equal to my height, and, after "reading" it, he folded it many times, made it a bracelet and put it on my hand.

"The paleness will go away, and you will be as red as this string," he said.

But it seems that my paleness was not jaundice, because it did not go away and I did not become at all as red as the string of the elderly exorcist.

On the other hand, the looking in kyra-Yiasemi's water left me for many years with a subconscious tendency—many times dangerous—to bend and look at my face in the wells and the lakes, the ponds, the buckets, even the stone troughs of the villages which were waiting full of cold water for the flocks to return from the field, to rush like crazy little children to quench their thirst, just as we used to rush in the good old days to the beloved sea of Kyrenia on the hot middays when the Nicosia bus would unload us students.

Now I don't have the strange subconscious tendency anymore, and I cannot tell when, how, and why it lost interest in the wet image of my face, when, how, and why I disappointed it and it abandoned me, which differently wrinkled face of mine disappointed it and it abandoned me, which differently wrinkled face of mine it is afraid of facing in the water.

My father remembered even Ayia Aikaterini. My mother had dedicated me to her grace at the time of my measles. She had said to me bringing me a little icon:

"I've brought you a saint to protect you" (She did not say to make you well lest I should think that I was in danger). "Look what a beautiful girl I chose for you!"

She was indeed very beautiful. I looked at her colorful icon in my fever with admiration.

"She has the same name as Katerinoula."

"Katerinoula my classmate?",

"Yes. Kiss her."

I kissed Ayia Aikaterini (I kissed Katerinoula) and I placed myself under her protection. My mother told me also the story of her life. She said that she was Jesus' "fiancée." It seems that I knew that people could get engaged from far away through a photograph (It had happened with a Greek American and a girl in our neighborhood. And after that, the photographers would ask the girls: "Do you want it for America?" "Why are you asking?" "So that I'll know what I'm doing"). So I was not interested in how the saint met with Christ. Moreover, I was attracted by the fact that the saint was a princess (just like in grandmother's fairy tales) and I cried filled with emotion when my mother narrated to me that they put her in a cauldron full of scalding tar and that nothing happened to her.

"It's probably not very hot," someone said.

And the saint threw a little bit with her finger to his face, which melted like a candle.

"We will celebrate her name day this year," said my father.

We always did. Only the past three or four years, with all our problems, had we neglected.

I was thinking: Why hadn't they got in time a saint for our Yiorgos and our Nikos? Why were they late remembering that?

So, grandmother had died a few years earlier. There still remains alive in my memory the autumn morning when I woke up and saw all my brothers and sisters gathered in my room. They were sitting silent and sullen. I looked questioningly.

"Grandmother died," they told me.

"Grandmother died?!"

They did not let us, the two young ones, out of the room. They brought us our breakfast there. And I did not cry. I don't know why, maybe because I was influenced by grandmother's narration of the death of afentis Batistas or maybe because I was facing it as a group and in company with my parents and siblings. And it was also the fact that they would not let me out of my room, as if telling me:

"It's not your responsibility!"

How was it not my responsibility? I was the one who the next day would go up the steps of the mezzanine (plaf, plaf, plaaaaf). "Hello, grandmother," and I would get no answer ("Welcome, my dear and tireless ears, welcome, voracious ears"), and I would find the bed unmade and the mezzanine empty.

So what if I did not cry? Something was happening inside me, something that, to this day, has preserved so vivid the announcement "Grandmother died" and the breakfast scene. Here I am chewing without any appetite the toasts and drinking the tea with sparse thoughtful gulps.

It was my first meeting with death. Not the death of the narrations, but the real death, our own death. And even though I saw it later cross our threshold repeatedly and take one time my brothers, another time my mother, another time my father, the two sisters, all young and not ripe for death, the first meeting has not been hurled far away, it still remains in my memory or somewhere else like a cloud, like a shadow, like I don' know what, however much I was not in a position to analyze it, however much I did not understand very well what it meant, except for the fact that I would not see grandmother again, I would not call her good morning again and I would hurriedly cross the corridor or even be afraid to cross it. Perhaps even, I could sense what beginning death was making, what dealings I would later on have with it, what war it would wage against me, what siege, which I would not face anymore as a group and in company but more and more alone, more and more alone.

The "later on" of the dealings of our family with death did not take long to come, as if someone were simply waiting for grandmother to open the account. For I was still in elementary school when, as I said—I return and narrate retrospectively—my two brothers, Yiorgos and Nikos, died three weeks apart from each other.

Yiorgos was a story which how can I omit even if my topic is different? He was the handsome and upstanding boy of the family and the neighborhood. The little girls gathered at our house to see him, tried to be friends with my sisters for his sake. And he was mother's favorite.

"You are all the same to me," she would say to forestall any complaint from us or to reassure her conscience.

No, we knew very well that we were not all the same to her. These things cannot hide and especially they cannot hide from children.

Did she love Yiorgos more because, beyond the instinct of a mother, who, I believe, turns her love toward the child who needs it the most, there is also something else inside her that has its own admirations? Because, at first glance, it was Nikos whom she should love more, the quiet, tender child who sanctified the house. She should love him more at least when at fifteen he was struck with leukemia and his neck was full of knots and he would button up his school uniform so that they would not show, until they could not be covered anymore and he was embarrassed to go to school and have his classmates ask him questions, and he stoically closed himself up at home and he would smile at us bitterly (he would smile at us a bitter, unbearable plaintiveness) and we knew that he was leaving us day by day. Perhaps, however, mother's instinct could sense that in the long run Yiorgos would need her love and care more despite his vitality. Perhaps her instinct knew that Nikos was a lost case while for Yiorgos there were hopes which had to be exhausted. As for me, the frailest, skinniest, the sickly and anemic leaf that was ready to fall with the first wind, it seems that I was not in real danger.

About our Nikos, I knew now that he would not again carry me on his back if I happened to fall again while coming home from kindergarten and scrape my knee and, touchy as I was, stay there for a long time waiting for him to get out of school so that he could carry me home.

I felt that he was deeply "indebted" to me and I was "collecting" implacably as soon as the slightest opportunity presented itself. And his deep "indebtedness" stemmed from the "cauterization" of my mole. It was a big mole on my left calf on a place which (I would call it edge) neither my shorts nor my sock could hide. A strange mole that got swollen and red when I was sad just like a little danger warning bulb. Yiorgos made the simile and the others liked it.

"Watch it! His little bulb will light!"

The women in the neighborhood would tell my mother:

"This is not a mole, it's a living thing, my kyra-Kalomoira. It must be an 'evil thing' that he caught in the baptismal font."

The doctor said that it was nothing, just an ordinary mole. An experienced midwife from Chrysopolitisa whom they called to see me said the same thing.

"Even if it's an 'evil thing,'" said the midwife, "it's for his own good. The dirty blood comes out."

(A doctor to whom my father had taken me to check my eyes, which used to get red, said something like that too: "It's his natural thing, don't worry. The eyes get cleaned!")

Finally my father brought a barber, Magianos, who could cure the "hair-eater." He applied the same cure to my mole as well. He scraped it with the splinter from a reed until it got bloody and he rubbed it with black wheat oil. I suffered stoically and didn't cry. Everything in vain. The mole returned a few days later just like a phoenix from his ashes. And then Nikos interfered.

"I will cauterize it for you and it will disappear," he said. "We learned at school."

I hesitated, I hesitated more, and I agreed.

"Will it hurt?"

"Well, it will hurt just for a moment, it can't be without pain."

We agreed to have the "cauterization" on a Thursday afternoon that we had no school. We kept it a secret from everyone.

And the agreed-upon Thursday came. We tried not to have anyone notice us, and went alone to a hiding place in the yard which was formed by two thick low-branched pomegranate trees. It was my refuge, where I went when they yelled at me or made me upset in play. I even had my little, wooden stool permanently there. And I would not answer when they called me so that they would be forced to come and find me and ask me:

"Who made you sad? Come on, let's go now."

So, I sat on the little stool, and Nikos took out of a bag the tool for the "cauterization," a piece of round iron. He also took out some pieces of charcoal, he gathered sticks, and lit them up. I was watching silently. I started getting scared. I was even more scared when I saw the iron become red-hot, burning, and gleaming. I got up.

"No, I don't want, I'm scared."

What was I scared of? He said this, he said that, and he convinced me.

I sat down on the stool again. My heart was pounding. Nikos could see that my fear was not completely gone.

"Shame on you. What kind of a man are you going to become? Look the other way. One little moment and we are done."

I looked the other way and he thrust the red-hot iron on my mole. Tsssssss!

I got up frantic with pain and screamed wildly.

"Owwww!"

I was crying, I was screaming, I was jumping.

Nikos was at a loss. He was screaming too:

"Mother!"

They heard us in the house and they ran.

My leg had melted. It smelled burned flesh.

"Holy Mary, my son!"

I stayed in bed for a month. I had horrible pains. The doctor was afraid that perhaps a permanent damage was done.

"It doesn't show yet. We'll see."

Everybody was distressed and most of all Nikos. As soon as he came home from school, he would run to ask me how I was and to keep me company. And he was in trouble both in the neighborhood and at school because what happened became known and they dubbed him "surgeon."

"Hello, surgeon! How is Mr. Surgeon?"

Nothing else occupied his mind except me and my leg. He would indulge my every wish obediently, and not just obediently, but gladly. He would pursue my wishes as if he felt a little lightened of the burden that he had on his conscience.

Father and mother saw him so distressed that they started worrying about him more than about me, especially since the days would go by and he would not calm down.

"He took it at heart. Let's hope nothing happens to him. He doesn't even care about school anymore."

Even if they scolded him a couple of times at the beginning, now they changed attitude completely and were comforting him.

"It's not your fault. How would you know? When you grow up, you'll remember it and laugh."

We would laugh? I did not agree and I took advantage of Nikos' guilt and tortured him as much as I could. And I would not even admit in front of him that I was better. I made him not know what to tell me. He was trying to put something on the other side of the scale.

"The mole will go away, you'll see."

I accepted his comfort with incredulity, cruelty, and fake indifference ("No, I'm not sparing you anything").

And I was right in my incredulity, because the mole did not go away. When the wound healed, it looked this way, it looked that way, it made sure there was no red-hot iron, and it popped out again and started quietly taking form as if nothing had happened. It even grew a little hair.

Yiorgos laughed and commented about the little hair:

"It's worse now. It has raised a flag to irritate the surgeon."

"Good sign," my mother would say when she saw me examining it. "God doesn't let it go away. When you put on long pants, they will hide it, and unseen it will work your good fortune."

In any case, even if the mole did not go away, at least there was no damage to my leg.

"Your surgeon is terrific!" I was being teased by the children and the women in the neighborhood, who found a conversation topic in the "cauterization" of my mole. "Come and tell us."

Even though I got well, I did not let Nikos off the hook. You are not off the hook easily when you owe to children. They do not even credit your payments. No loan shark measures up to them.

I let him off the hook only when illness struck him. And I let him off the hook in a heartbeat. I forgot about the burning and everything. And not only did I forget about it, but I was willing to sit again on the little stool of the hiding place on a Thursday afternoon and let him "cauterize" my mole again with the red-hot burning iron, if only the knots on his neck would go away.

"Come on, I'm not scared. This time it won't get away."

I felt that I was the one who owed now, and how would I pay off when he did not ask me to do even one little thing? Couldn't he understand my anxiety?

"Do you want anything, Nikos?"

"What could I want?"

"I don't know; just ask me for something."

And I was such a baby child that I reached the point to ask my mother one day:

"Is God punishing our Nikos for my mole? It didn't hurt that much. I faked it."

She hugged me crying.

And I don't know if it had anything to do with my remorse that, many years later, the picture of my father which I enlarged and put up in my office was the picture that he took for his passport when he was about to take Nikos to doctors in Cairo. The picture had such wrinkles of pain (that could not be enlarged more), had such grooves (that could not be excavated more), had such a horrible expression of anguish, had such a Nikos!

Even though all the time that Nikos was well, his account with me had a large debit balance, even though it was Nikos whom I waited for to carry me home on his back when I fell and scraped my leg ("Not you, Nikos, who owes me!"), my "protector" in the neighborhood and at school was Yiorgos.

"I'll tell Yiorgos!"

The threat was enough to protect me.

"He is Yiorgos' brother."

The "gangs" would come from Chrysopolitisa and the other "inland neighborhoods," as we scornfully called the neighborhoods up north, to jump and catch our "lingri" stick in the air provoking us (just as older boys would provoke if they stole a girl of ours), to cut the strings of our kites, or to hide and aim at us with slings.

Yiorgos would chase them up to their dens. Once, while chasing them, he jumped into the yard of the house of their leader, who hid terrified in the kitchen. His mother screamed at Yiorgos.

"Get out, you bum, before I call the police. What a nerve!"

"I have every right," said Yiorgos. "Control your honey boy."

"Get lost, you and your rights. If it were not for your father…."

The women in the neighborhood ran, and Yiorgos left threatening:

"Tell your scoundrel to gather his belt because I will catch him outside and take care of him."

It seems that he had heard that in the villages when someone was looking for a fight he would leave his belt dragging so that someone might step on it and thus give him an excuse.

The boy's mother did not understand:

"What belt are you talking about, you bum?"

The neighbors told her to report the case to the police.

"Report what? We know these things already. His father will take care of it, and he will be our enemy on top of it."

And she took it out on her son, who had come out shy and ashamed:

"What did you do to him? Why do you fight with him? Don't you see what a wild cat he is? I'll tell your father and he will take care of you."

Yiorgos was also the referee in the rooster fights we held secretly in the "Big Field." However deserted from houses the "Big Field" was, just to be on the safe side we would stand in a circle and create a wall lest a passer-by might see. These were the "local," the "semi-final," so to speak, rooster fights. We would secretly take the roosters from our houses, and hide them under our coats to take them to fight at the "Big Field." They would wiggle, scratch at us, take their heads out, and we would push them back in. At the local meets we would not let the roosters get killed. As soon as it was clear which one was the strongest and most stubborn and fierce, we would stop the fight and take the wounded roosters back to the coop. Our mothers would see them the next day and wonder.

"Look at that plucked rooster. The hens must have beaten him up. Who knows what he did."

Being women, they were saying it perhaps with some satisfaction, with a certain pious inward thought about the possibility of its application to the human race as well.

When the winner of the "semi-finals" was proclaimed, we called the "inlands" to bring their own rooster for a final match. The "Big Field" would fill up with children, a double, triple, impenetrable wall.

A sparse passer-by might wonder.

"Why have so many children gathered here today?"

Yiorgos and the representative of the "inlands" would walk to the middle of the circle with the roosters in their arms and greet each other.

"Hello, Yiorgos."

"Hello, Yiannis."

They would shake hands and let the roosters free.

One time the final match was almost cancelled, because the boy could not get the candidate rooster of the neighborhood the night before. It was not even dawn yet when he came and woke up Yiorgos.

"I can't. The hens are making a lot of noise. My father woke up too and checked. Fortunately I managed to hide."

Yiorgos always had a recipe. In this case he advised like an experienced hen-thief:

"Go naked into the coop, and you'll see that the hens won't make a sound. Do I have to tell you everything?"

And that's what happened. The hens were quiet. And the wrestler was kidnapped, and the final match took place.

"Really, how come the hens kept quiet?" we asked.

"Because, since he was naked, they took him for a big strange animal and they were scared," replied Yiorgos.

Now, if I alone paid for our cruel games, it was unfair, because being such a little child, I had no real involvement whatsoever. And it should be to my credit that when the others were chasing the crickets, I was begging them crying not to catch them.

My punishment came from our big rooster. Alas for me if he was out of the coop and I happened to go out to the yard. He would fly and sit on my head, as if he were pointing at me.

"He is the one responsible!"

I was forced to ask for an escort in order to go out.

"The child will catch jaundice from his fear. We should slaughter that rooster," said my mother.

They were trying not to take him out of the coop at all, and the rooster would get angry and go up and down and scratch on the wires and scream and protest when he saw the hens strolling freely while he was kept prisoner.

"You are dancing on your grave, rooster-brained. Easter will be here soon," my father would say.

One day, while they were opening the coop to let the hens out, the rooster managed to get out too. He went up on the clay oven looking magnificent, shook his wings and shouted triumphantly his victory so that his subordinates could hear and, at the same time, we would be piqued. Father was offended and chased him. It was a wild chase. They went around the yard five times. We stood and watched just as the Trojans watched Achilles and Hector. Father realized that his stories about his adventures in Transvaal and in the Troodos forest were at risk in our eyes. He was out of breath, but he did not give in. Finally he caught the rooster.

"You worthless one!"

He didn't know what to do with him. A rooster cannot take blows with a stick, or punches. In his helplessness father started slapping him on the head. Having no resistance, the head was going back and forth, and the rooster did not seem to mind the slaps. It was a funny scene. We all laughed. Father turned and looked at us angrily.

"What are you laughing about? Do you see anything funny?"

"Do we ever see something funny!"

I proposed a solution to Yiorgos:

"Why don't we take him to fight?"

I said that with the hope that he would get killed.

"He's not for fights. He's big and old. Don't judge from the fact that he's fighting with you. He has no guts to get out on the plaza."

"He has guts. Didn't you see them? Very big ones."

Yiorgos laughed.

"Not guts of old age. It takes a different kind of guts."

"Did you see the crest?"

"The crest is just for strutting."

"Then let him be defeated," I said in retort, "so that we'll get rid of him."

Yiorgos did not like that.

"Let him be defeated so that we'll get rid of him? And what about the honor of the house and the honor of the neighborhood?"

However much we knew that mother loved Yiorgos most of all, we did not mind because we were at the age when we admire upstandingness, for different reasons the boys and the girls, the former ones because in its model they see their own deficiencies being completed, the latter because they weave around it the dream of the beloved one they are waiting for.

So when Yiorgos went to the English School in Nicosia, the house became empty for all of us and we anxiously waited for Saturday when he would come home.

What incredible homecomings! Some twenty six miles by bike.

"From Nicosia to Skala by bike?"

He would ring his bicycle bells from far away and the girls would come out on the balconies and the kiosks, and the doors would open and the little children would stop their games. They could distinguish the ringing.

"Yiorgos!"

They would circle the bike. A bike was not at all a common thing back then and even less common was such a beautiful bike like the one Yiorgos had, with so many trimmings and accessories: two big, shining bells—we called them "twins"—one was deep-voiced and the other one tenor and playful (and Yiorgos would

61

coordinate them with the bells of Ayios Lazarus' church), two round little mirrors on the right and left of the handlebars, an electric flashlight at the front and red reflectors on the rear fender and the pedals. There was also usually a thick bracelet of jasmine on the brake bar.

"Wow, what a bike!"

The first time that I studied it, after the completion of the inspection, I asked Yiorgos:

"Doesn't it have a crank so that it can go faster?"

"A what?"

"A crank."

I remembered when we were traveling once by carriage from Paphos to Limassol. We were exhausted and as soon as we reached the station, I sat on a stone block and did not want to get up.

"I'll stay here, mama, please."

When the carriage started again, they lifted me up and had me sit next to the coachman so that I wouldn't whine.

The coachman caressed me, smiled at me and said:

"Do you see this crank? When I turn it, the carriage goes faster. Don't worry."

And he turned the crank, and it seemed to me that indeed the carriage was going faster. So many years have passed, and even though I don't have, unfortunately, anymore the old childlike innocence, curiously I still believe that with the turn of the crank the carriage did indeed go faster.

In the same way something of my childhood terror returns in a certain form when I remember the wax figure of San Luccio in the basement of the monastery of the Nuns lying down in his coffin with the red wound on his face. So much so, that, as a grown up, I was not impressed by the mummies of the pharaohs in the Cairo Museum, and I would tell my children:

"You should have seen San Luccio!"

I would not want (nor would I be able) to enter into psychological interpretations, but at least these were real memories (albeit curiously intense, which were each time engorged in order to confront the things that might be threatening to undermine them). Inexplicable were the memories that I had of things that did not take place. I insisted, for example, that when I was a very young child, before my first memory of grandmother, that is two or three years old, I was traveling once by train with my mother and father. Next to us there was sitting a Turkish woman with a veil on, and my mother had her lap full of peanuts and we were all picking some. In fact at a stop my father got me down to take me to the bathroom and we almost missed the train.

However much my father contradicted me, however much my mother contradicted me, I could see the scene very much alive in front of me and I insisted. Anyway, my mother noted the presence of the Turkish veiled woman, for I don't know why a veiled woman in dreams meant—strange identification—the Holy Mary.

"The Holy Mary was sending you a message. She is still sending you something good that she doesn't reveal to us."

"And the peanuts that the Turkish woman was picking from your lap?"

"I don't know about that" (You don't know? You will find out later, mother, we will find out later, mother).

Another strange memory is that one day I saw some small swallows that were flying very high up in the sky over our neighborhood and that everybody said they were German planes.

"German planes had not come to Cyprus during the First World War," everybody would tell me.

"But they did," I insisted. "I saw them. Everybody in the neighborhood saw them."

Anyway, it was about the crank of the carriage of Paphos that I was asking Yiorgos. And as for the carriage, I was saving my pennies to buy it. I was giving them to my mother:

"Save them for me so that I can buy the carriage of Paphos."

A breeze of life, a March tree-swell breeze that brings the knots to the branches, was rushing every Saturday into the house. The preparations were starting at daybreak with a strange fever. And for lunch we would eat our favorite food, ravioli, which my mother would not make any other day because it took too long and was a lot of work.

"Thanks to the basil the flowerpot drinks water too," my brothers and sisters whispered secretly so that my mother would not hear and be sad.

And secretly again:

"To the health of the basil!"

Even though my mother could not hear, I could, and one day, not knowing what I was doing, I said aloud:

"To the health of the basil!"

Everybody turned and looked at me. Mother and father strangely, the others reproachfully.

In the afternoon and on Sunday the girls in the neighborhood would suddenly miss my sisters and come to see them.

At some point Yiorgos finished the English School and got a job in Nicosia and did not come to Skala but rarely.

"He has adjusted to living in Nicosia," we would say. "He has made friends."

We didn't know that it was not like that, that it was not like that at all, that it was because he had fallen in love in Nicosia.

He fell in love with a blond young girl in the narrow streets of Royiatiko. A young girl who was not mature enough, who at sixteen could not be mature enough, for a faithful love. And one day Yiorgos found the blond girl with someone else.

In despair, he quit his job and returned to Skala. He told us everything with a childlike plaintiveness ("Why plaintiveness? Is that how upstandingness is lost from one moment to the next? How come he did not smash the face of his rival like the face of the "inlands?" Were our kites worth more?").

He said that he was finished with Nicosia. He would leave for Athens to study.

Mother was crying, we sulked. It was the time of the great disaster in Asia Minor.

"Your mother will die," said father. "Is this time for studies? Don't you see that we are under fire from Turkey? Let's wait and see first what will happen."

"My mother won't die, father. I will die if I stay."

Father was then Assistant Commander and when he saw that Yiorgos would not change his mind, he simply forbade it:

"I won't give you a passport. You can swim to Athens!"

What? He would not give him a passport? What right did he have? Father did not know his son well, he did not know him well at all. Yiorgos wrote to the Colonial Secretary, who issued father a service reprimand and an order to issue a passport.

"He reported me, Kalomoira, do you understand?" father was telling mother. "He reported his parent. I don't want to ever see him again!"

"If you say that again, I will die."

And father never said it again, and he saw him again.

"Your passport is ready. Come and sign and you'll get it."

Yiorgos took father's hand and held it and squeezed it.

And he left and the horrible drama of the house started and the telegrams started coming in:

"Send money; sick."

The conversations between father and mother are still alive deep inside me while he was shaving before leaving for the office. My mother was not asking, she was begging like a little child so much that now that I think of her it hurts me that I was not older so that I would be able to give her the money that her Yiorgos was asking for.

"Take it, mother, and let father be. Father doesn't know about these things."

My father had his objections.

"He is lying, Kalomoira, he is not sick. Where is he spending all the money that I'm sending him?"

"And what if he is not lying? What if it's true?"

And the money was leaving, and the telegrams were coming in again:

"Send money; sick."

And again the same conversation between father and mother, and again the money was leaving (Father, the money you were sending him was not enough to make him forget).

The house was breathing heavily with the head bowed. And Yiorgos was really sick, he was not lying. He came to us suddenly and unexpectedly. He was pale and a mere skeleton. We were terrified. Was this Yiorgos? We were terrified and at the same we screamed with joy just as when he would come on his bike from Nicosia.

"You didn't ring the twins so that we could hear you," we said.

He smiled.

"No twins anymore".

He said that he had tuberculosis. He comforted us.

"I didn't come here to die; I came to you to get well."

And mother said:

"Of course you'll get well, my son. No question about it."

I see him again lying in the armchair with his blank foggy look. They told us, the youngest children, not to go near. They found an excuse:

"It's not right. He gets tired. Sick people get tired with children. He needs complete quiet."

So we avoided chatting with him. We would just smile at him as we were passing by in front of him. And all day long we would pass by as if we were flirting with him, as if to replace the approach.

"Quiet, he is sleeping."

One day he beckoned me to go near. I looked around to make sure he was beckoning to me ("Yes, it was to me") and I ran and knelt near him happy that he chose me. No one dared tell me openly: "Don't go." I knew it and I threw them a triumphant look ("Stop me if you can!").

"Do you remember grandmother's stories?" he asked.

"Of course I remember them!"

He remained thoughtful for a moment.

"How beautiful it was back then!"

However much he was sick, I did not let him off the hook (Children do not let off the hook easily):

"It's a pity that you grown-ups thought she was exaggerating."

"No, she was not exaggerating at all. You are right."

Then he changed the subject.

"How are the bums the 'inlands'?"

"New ones are out in the plaza."

And I cannot forget the episode with the half shilling. He had given it to me to split with Chrystalla, my immediately older sister. We changed it at the grocer's and got four and a half grosia. The grocer could not break the half grosi into two ten-para pieces. We asked around, but nobody had change. Frustrated, we went back to the grocer and gave him back the four and a half grosia.

"Give us back our half shilling."

We took it to Yiorgos.

"You couldn't split it?"

"No. It's okay."

He smiled. And we smiled too. Then he laughed loudly, so much that he choked from coughing. Mother ran worried.

It was the time when people were terrified of the horrible disease. Neither the girls in the neighborhood nor his friends came to see him. He understood, and he did not ask.

I can still hear his cough, nails in my chest.

"Listen, he is coughing again."

"Was he coughing last night, mama?"

"No. He slept well" (How can you say "he slept well" and cry, mother?).

Then:

"If God wants, can He stop the cough, mama?"

"Of course. In a heartbeat."

"And Yiorgos can become like before?"

"Like before and better."

I can still see the blood that he spat. It terrified me so much that years later, every time I spat, it became a habit to me to check if I had spat blood. As a student in high school and then at the university, when the others at the camps and field trips would indifferently spit on the ground, I always carried, even if I was naked in the sun, a handkerchief so that I could spit in it.

"Bravo! Good manners," they would make fun of me.

I would not open it in front of others. I would hide it with fake indifference and check to make sure no one was looking before I opened it.

And I was in my second year at the university in Athens when one day, after a tiring cough for two weeks, I spat blood in my handkerchief. I was terrified. I folded the handkerchief and, holding it tight in my hand like an amulet, like a secret message, like I don't know what, I ran home. On the way suddenly everything seemed fake and foreign. My landlady saw me agitated.

"What happened?" she asked me worried. "Is something wrong?"

"No, nothing."

I locked myself in my room and unfolded the handkerchief slowly as if it were a little bird that might fly away.

I kept touching the blood with my finger, I wanted to talk with it, I kept looking at the fibers and its penetrations in the plegm (A midwife from Korvos or an old man from Avlakia might be able to read your fortune and your future in the penetrations, just like in the lines in the palm, even better actually because these were coming alive from inside you).

Yiorgos' drama was shaking me again in a strange way. I was almost finding pleasure in the misfortune that was foreboded.

The next morning I went to see the doctor at the university student center secretly from my friends and fellow students. He ordered an x-ray and a saliva test. He saw me upset and gave me courage:

"It's nothing, don't worry."

At the hospital where he sent me I had the bad luck to run into an acquaintance of mine from Cyprus who was a medical student. He was puzzled.

"What are you doing here? Are you sick?"

"I have trouble going up the stairs and uphill," I said. "The doctor is waiting for me."

The x-ray did not show anything. And neither did the saliva test. I took the paper with the results and went to the bathroom to open it. I opened that one also slowly, just like my handkerchief. Negative.

"I just see a swelling of the glands," the doctor said. "Do you eat well?"

And something that definitely goes back to Yiorgos' illness (and later mother's) is the fact that, since the time they told us at school (I don't know how they got the idea) that rabbits are prone to tuberculosis, I have never eaten rabbit again, with the subconscious fear that I might eat something that had to do with Yiorgos and my mother.

Once I saw Yiorgos in the storage room looking at his bike and caressing it. He even rang the "twins." How that ring sounded! And how much my mother secretly cried. And we were unable to help our Yiorgos since his illness was not some "inland" neighborhood boy.

The doctor gave him a series of injections and ordered rest. He preferred a combination of mountain and sea.

"Is Lapithos okay?"

Yes, Lapithos was exactly what he needed.

Irinia took him, because my mother had Nikos sick and could not leave him.

I don't know how many examples of sisterly self-sacrifice like Irinia's there are. She was his nurse; always with him, washing his face and his hands, changing his bloody handkerchiefs, giving him his medications, reading the newspaper to him, and even feeding him, not feeding him, eating with him from the same plate, with the same spoon and the same fork.

"There is nothing wrong with you, my Yiorgos."

However much my father would scold her, she wouldn't listen.

"I don't get sick."

The neighborhood would get angry with our family.

"They let a tender girl!" (What a debt you debited us, my sister, what sisters you made out of the sisters of the whole world!)

They went to some relatives of my father's in Lapithos, but a few days later they came back. It was a dramatic return.

"They threw us out," said Irinia. "They found out about Yiorgos' illness and they kicked us out. They threw our suitcases out in the street."

She was crying. Tired from the long trip and the horrible experience and deeply hurt, Yiorgos stood there looking at us with withered and plaintive eyes. Mother hugged him.

"Don't be sad, my dearest son, don't be sad, my brave boy, that's how people are. We'll all go together to Lefkara, where they love us."

Then, other telegrams started coming in from Athens.

"I loaned your son one hundred drachmas. Please wire."

"I loaned your son two hundred drachmas. Please wire."

"I loaned your son…." "I loaned your son…."

We would show them to Yiorgos to approve or not approve the payment:

"He is telling the truth."

"He is lying."

One day his suitcase, which they had kept in Alexandria, was sent home. He was very happy and thanked father for paying and taking care of it. He had many little things and letters inside, and he would look through them for a long time.

Yiorgos died about a month later. In his wallet we found the picture of the unfaithful blond girl of the Royiatiko.

"Bitch!" said father.

Mother was silent. She was looking at it—she was looking at it as if she were seeing something of her Yiorgos, and she hid it lest we should tear it up.

"Yiorgos didn't tear it up. We won't either."

As a grown up, I felt a strange bond with the Royiatiko. At the Royiatiko I would spend my vacation, at the Royiatiko I lived when I got my first job, the Royiatiko was going around in my verses.

"What bonds do you have with the Royiatiko?" they would ask me.

"Yiorgos."

"Yiorgos who?"

"My brother."

"You have a brother?"

"I had."

"You had a brother?"

"Of course. Did you think they brought me down in a basket?"

I would say that as if I could not have been born without a brother, as if I could not have been born without Yiorgos.

It was strange what attracted me to the Royiatiko. What was I looking for anyway? To fall in love with a blond girl and live Yiorgos again and sink in his melancholy, or to take revenge? And how would I take revenge? And on whom?

The horrible days when we were losing our Yiorgos were brought again alive and bleeding in front of me forty-five years later by an old woman at the Land Registry Office in Kyrenia.

"Are you Costakis?" she asked me when she heard the clerk call my name.

"Yes, why?"

"I'm an aunt of yours from Lapithos."

Aunt? I was disconcerted. Was she the one who threw Yiorgos out in the street?

She told me her name. She was the one. Half a century suddenly became yesterday. Here is the dramatic return from Lapithos. Here is Yiorgos, hurt and exhausted, looking at me.

I got very upset. I talked to her harshly. She was surprised that I knew and remembered those things.

"Forget them? I drag them like lead, like a rope around my neck."

She listened impassively, she let me finish, and then her words stabbed me like a knife:

"Do you know that I had a baby and that he died shortly after from tubercular meningitis? I'm not saying, of course...."

I was torn to shreds. And I told her absurdly and supposedly unyieldingly:

"You could at least find a better way."

Since the subject was coming back, I had to weigh whether my father was right in hiding Yiorgos' illness from her. I had to put myself in his place, a gaping precipice in front of him and having no other choice. I don't know....

About the blond girl, I found out who she was and unwittingly watched her life.

She was married with children and I was a university student when I met her one summer in Morphou. I did not bear any resemblance to Yiorgos, and still I found out that she was asking who I was, she was strangely asking who I was. And when they told her my name, she was disturbed.

She used to know a Yiorgos Montis long time ago, she said. What was he to him?

"He doesn't have any brothers, I don't know if he did."

Twenty days after our Yiorgos, Nikos left us too. The house was shaking to its foundations. Mother was a living dead. She closed herself up in the kitchen surrounded by the poor women of the neighborhood. She did not care about us at all. As if it were our fault. Many times she would even leave us without any bread while she would wrap in a napkin the bread that my father used to get with a food-card and she would send me to take it secretly sometimes to one family, sometimes to another.

"To kyra-Katina. To old-Hatzina."

"I'll take it, mama."

It was the secret that joined me with my mother, the private secret bond that the others did not have and that flattered me immensely.

I would run happily to report to her that I had accomplished the mission:

"I took it, mama."

She would kiss me and give me the greatest wish one could make:

"Have my blessing and I pray that one day you'll become a bishop."

I didn't like the wish and I was praying for it not to come true. I told her one day:

"Mama, I don't want to become a bishop."

"To have them kiss your hand?"

"No." (Why should they kiss my hand, mother? What ideas were those that you were suggesting to me?)

She smiled a bitter smile, as much as was still left to her.

"Why didn't you tell me? Okay, we'll change the wish."

"And the old ones that you gave me?"

"I'll take them back, don't worry about that."

"Don't forget any, okay?"

"No, I won't forget."

I stared at her penetratingly (did you notice how penetratingly children stare?) trying to see if I was making her sad by rejecting the bishop's position.

"Unless you want it very much, mama."

"No, I was just saying it."

In the evening my father would be surprised when he would see just a few thin slices of bread on the table:

"Don't we have any more bread?"

"No."

"That's strange."

I would keep my mouth shut.

One day I tripped and fell. The bread was revealed and rolled on the street, my secret was revealed and rolled exposed on the street.

Even though my knees were bleeding, I didn't care (as I always used to care so much about every little scratch). I ran terrified and grabbed the bread in my arms.

My mother saw me bleeding and was worried.

"What happened, my baby?"

I did not answer. I wiped the blood indifferently with my hand and gave my report:

"I took it, mama."

Once I found a lira on the street. It was folded in four in an empty cigarette pack. I ran happily to take it to my mother:

"For my piggy bank for the carriage."

She thought for a moment.

"What if a poor person lost it?"

Poor? Ah, yes, she was right. Someone poor must have lost it for sure, the way it was folded in the cigarette pack.

"I suggest that we give it away for the souls of Yiorgos and Nikos."

I agreed on one condition: that it would be from me.

"Of course it's from you, my son. They can see."

"It's better to say it so that they can hear."

"Okay, I'll say it."

For the souls of Yiorgos and Nikos, she was also filling up her closet with beaded handbags. They were beautiful, heavy, colorful handbags. I asked her.

"The Russian refugees make them," she told me.

"Refugees? What are refugees?"

She tried to explain and gave me the impression that we were going back to grandmother's fairy tales, because she talked to me about princes and princesses who now worked at the cafeterias and restaurants and sang and played the piano and washed dishes.

Unfortunately none of the beaded handbags survived in the house, and I don't know if their designs had something of their distant longed-for country, something of their mansions and the decorations and the colorful lights they lived in.

Father saw the handbags one day.

"What are all these handbags?"

Mother did not reply. She shut the closet abruptly and stood in front of it like a little child with open arms to protect it.

My father smiled sweetly and sadly.

Saturday was the only day that mother would go out; she would take her bath at the hamam and later take flowers to the cemetery. The combination was completely coincidental. It just so happened that Saturday was as much the day for a bath as it was for a visit to the cemetery.

(Taking a bath once a week was the most you could expect back then in the towns of the island. In the villages, if you asked how often they took a bath, they might answer boastfully: "Very often. Every single Easter." And of course, there were some priests who never took a bath "lest the holy myrrh should be washed away!")

Mother's companion both at the hamam and at the cemetery was always I, probably because I was, after all, the only son left to her.

At the hamam all the women took little boys, children or brothers, before they started being curious about the nakedness that surrounded them. So my mother used to take me too until one day the Turkish scrubbing woman suspected me even though I was small and shy. So she told my mother to stop taking me with her to the hamam.

"Let him come at night with your husband, *hanım*."

"Why?" wondered my mother. "He is *çocuk*."

"*Çocuk*, but do you see how his eyes look at women?"

I watched the dialogue and begged my mother not to tell the reason why she would not take me again with her to the hamam. And I even said that I would not go with my father.

"Who told you to go? We'll be washing you at home."

"I want *you* to be washing me, not my sisters."

"I will, don't worry."

But she did not wash me like before, she had no spirit, she had no strength, she would forget. And one day, the barber found a louse in my hair. He showed it to me. I blushed and left running.

At home I did not say a word. I hid in my hiding place and cried.

Mother would not even sit at the table with us. Father, on the other hand, would try to numb his grief with the pain of the refugees from Asia Minor who were flooding the island and more and more were arriving in every kind of boat. There was not a single hole in Skala that was not filled with the tragic flood. Soon the diseases started too. So much so that in the end the Government was forced to prohibit any more people from disembarking. So the boats would stay a few days hesitant and undecided and then they would start again and leave in despair. But there was one caique that wouldn't leave.

"It doesn't go any farther," said the captain. "We barely made it up to here."

The British Commander did not believe that. Besides, he had strict orders from Nicosia.

"I'm sorry. I can see no way to help."

Father got on the caique two or three times together with the commander and he would come home and tell us about it, especially tell mother about it.

"You should see all that misery, Kalomoira!"

They were all women and children on the caique. The people found about it too and were sending food and clothing. They knew the "no" and the stubbornness of the British and didn't hope but to look one morning and not to see the caique in the harbor. To no avail. The caique was still there like a nightmare over the town.

The commander would get angry.

"Still there!"

And suddenly father lifted the nightmare off the chest of the town. He took advantage of the commander's tour in the province and gave permission and the passengers of the caique came out. They were pouring out like crazy and kissing the ground. Who could gather them now?

"I let them out, Kalomoira!"

His eyes filled with tears.

"May the souls of Yiorgos and Nikos find peace."

The commander flew into a rage.

"You stupid!"

Father (for the first time in his life) accepted the insult silently.

"I'll report you to the Colonial Secretary!"

And he reported him. My father was summoned by the Colonial Secretary in Nicosia to apologize. And he apologized:

"I apologize. I lost two sons in twenty days. One of them was the one to whom you ordered me to issue a passport. Do you remember? When I saw the children on the caique, my mind became foggy and stopped working. I didn't know what I was doing."

The Colonial Secretary accepted the apology. He even said:

"I am sorry about your children. About the passport, you realize that I was not allowed to handle it differently."

Some of the women of the caique were added to my mother's circle of friends. They would come to see her and tell her about their own drama and to comfort her.

"Look at the courage that we have."

With the difference that after some time my mother got jealous of Zenovia (how the names are coming back as if I were taking notes!), a beautiful blond and sweet-talking young woman whose husband the Turks had slaughtered before her eyes.

"I don't know, find a way to tell her," she told father shyly.

And father was flattered to see that she was still able to get jealous, that through her horrible tragedy she was able to be jealous of him. He was flattered and at the same time he had some encouraging thoughts:

"Good sign."

(By the way, what happened to Zenovia? What wish of my mother's did I respect and I never sought her? Because, what can I say, I think that mother should be more jealous of Zenovia and me, the way I would look at her silently in the eyes and feel a shiver going through me, the way her eyes had swept away my first teacher in kindergarten, and Froso, the little girl in my neighborhood, and Katerinoula, my classmate.)

I remember very well the refugees from Asia Minor, Greeks and Armenians. All they managed to bring with them were their gold jewelry and some gold coins. They sold them and, being creative and hard workers, they thought of all kinds of jobs that the locals did not do or did not know about. At the corners they set up little stores that could fix anything we used to throw away until then, the streets were filled with Greek–Turkish voices of peddlers who could do this and that and the other, and they started newly-emerging industries. It was a boost and a push which may have not yet been appreciated as much as it should. To us children, most impressive was the refugee confectionery that made candy.

"It makes candy!"

It was not easy seeing candy being made in our place. We would gather and admire the big cauldron that was going round and round. The candy maker's son was a classmate of mine. And we would ask him:

"Do you also know how to make bicycles?"

He would laugh. No, they didn't.

Even though they did not know how to make bicycles, they knew how to make a lot of other things and, in our area of interest, smart toys and beautiful dolls.

However, I believe that I should mention here an episode whose main character was justified fifty years later. When a middle-aged woman saw from the caique a minaret in Skala, she got upset:

"There are Turks here too? I'm not getting down."

They would explain to her in vain that the British ruled the island.

"No matter who rules it, the Turks will one day do what they did to us."

So, on her insistence, they put her on another caique that was going to Greece.

(With regard to the refugees from Asia Minor who came to Cyprus, it should be added that, even though they had actually no help from the colonial government, they never knew poverty neither did any of them live in a shed nor was any girl forced to go astray, as had happened in Greece. And the reasons must be the incomparably larger number of refugees who went to Greece, the post–war bleeding wounds of Greece as a state and as economy, and the wide margins for diverse activities that existed on an underdeveloped island such as Cyprus was at the time).

That tragic period was brought alive again before my adult eyes by a sweet old woman from Chios who was among the refugees who had come from Greece in 1942 to escape the hunger of the German occupation.

"It's the second time that I come as a refugee to Cyprus," she told me. "I also came twenty years ago to Skala and I wish I had stayed rather than let the relatives take me with them."

(Why do you wish you had stayed, my little old woman? How do you know that you would have time to die before the Turks came here too?)

The Russian refugees were something else. They did not know any trade, they did not have the knotty hands of the Asia Minor people, they had brought nothing with them but the air of the parlors and their civilization, and they became, as I said, singers and musicians and waiters. It was a different influence on the provincialism of the island. And if they made the beaded handbags that I mentioned, they were just a kind of cultural activity, which could have been paintings if there were in Cyprus at the time such a broad buying public for paintings as there was for handbags. The songs of the Russian refugee aristocrats were importing for the first time in Cyprus excerpts from foreign operettas. And since Skala gathered together the culture of the island and was virtually the capital, since all the consulates were there, and, together with Limassol, was an entry point for the European civilization, it provided fertile ground for Lehar and Coleman, whom you could hear now on the pianos of homes, on the guitars of the cantada singers, and the quiet songs of the "ponte" and the "boulevard."

And of course there was no communist party then on the island, which might oppose the presence of the "fugitives" and create problems for them.

The other difference with the Russians is that they did not stay on the island like the people from Asia Minor. And they did not leave behind but a couple of girls who had married Cypriots, and a dancer, Larista, who, well into her old age, was going around the theaters and the clubs and was teaching choreography. I remember when I was writing for the "Lyriko," she asked me to translate a favorite Russian song of hers, the "Yamcshik" (ямщик, coachman):

> *Yamcshik, my coachman, don't go fast,*
> *I don't have much distance anymore,*
> *I'm not going to find love,*
> *Yamcshik, my life is closed.*

And I remember the Russian pianist who accompanied the silent series at the "Paté" theater: the "Yellow Sphere," the "Ace of Diamonds," the "Rokemball," the "Freedom." A woman—also Russian—used to sit close to him and the pianist would turn his head and they would chat endlessly. He would just glance at the screen once in a while and readjust his music. And if he happened to forget himself in some slow, sad notes while the "hero" was running unrestrained on the horse to save the girl, the woman would nudge him abruptly, and he would hit crazy galloping octaves!

For me Yiorgos' death from tuberculosis had one more complication. My friends moved away from me. I myself even heard a classmate of mine, Antonis, tell them:

"Don't go near him, he may have tuberculosis."

I left school running and fell into my mother's lap crying. She was scared.

"What's wrong, my baby? Are you sick?"

I told her:

"I wish Yiorgos were alive. He would show them!"

And I don't know what connection (if any) the episode had with my behavior two years later. One day I had an argument with a neighborhood boy whose father had been sentenced to prison for embezzlement, and I shouted at him:

"You go and find your father in prison!"

He left with his head bent down without answering. And he must have fallen, just as I (more than I) had before, into his mother's lap crying.

For half a century I've had on my conscience the stab that I gave him. A stab which became more painful when, some fifteen years later, I found out that he was in an asylum. I went to see him. I found him in the yard as tame as a little lamb building little houses with mud. I talked to him, he didn't recognize me. I reminded him, he could not remember. He was looking at me curiously ("Who was I?").

Who was I? I realized that there was no way anymore to unburden my conscience.

I sat next to him to build little houses, I sat to play again together like before. He was smiling at me, and his smile was slaughtering me.

"I'll come again," I told him when I was leaving.

"Yes," he replied.

But I did not go again. I did not go even though I knew that I was adding more pain than taking away. Because, for sure, he must have been waiting for me.

Four years after Yiorgos' and Nikos' death, mother died too of "rapidly progressing" tuberculosis. It seems that she got the same illness (and "rapidly progressing" so that she would not delay) as her Yiorgos, fearing that, if she died in a different way, she might not be able to find him.

When she was seriously ill and it was obvious that it was not pneumonia, as the doctors had surmised at the beginning, my father took me to Lefkara, the village on the mountains where we used to spend happy times in the summers. Father used to rent a fig tree for each one of us, and we would go every afternoon, when the mountain sides were shadowed (how beautiful the afternoon shadows of the mountain sides!), and we would each gather the fruit from our own fig tree and bring home the figs and spread them out so that they would become "dried." And we took such good care of our figs, waiting to see whose would become better! We would put them on a string and make necklaces and we would tie a little piece of paper with our name: Irinia, Elengo, Yiorgos, Nikos, Chrystalla, Costakis. Since the first few years the others had to write my name, I did not trust them and I would ask my mother:

"What does it say?"

"Costakis."

"Are you sure?"

"I'm sure."

"Read it again so that I can hear it."

We would hide them separately, and in the winter we would eat them sparingly and with planning lest ours should finish while the others would still have some.

When the necklaces of the figs were naked strings, we would start on the carobs. Carobs were a cheap substitute and they would not apportion them to us. They just kept them loose in a big cloth bag hanging in the storage room and we were all free to stick our hands in and get some.

"Whatever we get out of the bucket!" we would say.

We used to make fun of the one whose figs had run out:

"I guess tomorrow you will start on the carobs."

I don't know why we thought so little of the carobs, which were otherwise chosen by father, big, thick and full of honey and sugar. Did we already know—even I—about the "prodigal son" who was eating carobs?

We even had little fights about the figs and complaints to mother.

"Where did Chrystalla find the figs? She had run out. She must have taken some of mine."

"I hadn't run out, I was pretending. I had some hidden elsewhere."

"Let me see the paper. Does it say 'Chrystalla,' mother?"

How different Lefkara was then.

"Don't you want a fig tree?" father asked me hesitantly.

"No, I don't." (What a question, father!)

And every day we waited anxiously for news about mother. There are some new injections, they told us. An Armenian doctor recommended them. Tomorrow they will give her the first one.

"My Ayia Aikaterini," I would pray in the evenings, "forget about me and save my mama."

The news was coming in a letter that Hoppas would bring us on his carriage. A trip with Hoppas was a tragedy since the four horses could not go up the hill the last four curves and the passengers had to get down so that the carriage would be lighter and sometimes (many times) they even had to push.

When they were on flat ground again, Hoppas would sit again proudly on his high seat:

"Come on, everyone get in! Let's go!"

He would pass like the wind through the narrow gravel roads of the village with a haughty victorious "hoppa" which, with time, became his nickname. The "hoppa" proclaimed throughout the village:

"We ate up the uphill road again."

They would hear him from far away and run and pick up whatever was left in the street.

"Hoppas!"

He would wave his whip clanging up to the basils on the balconies ("Hello, basils!") and many times he had carried with him chairs and tables, for in his triumphant entry, how could he stop for a little table or a chair?

My brothers and sisters and I knew about his entry into Skala because his "garage" was a "big grove" near our house. We, the little children in the neighborhood, would run to welcome him as soon as we heard him from far away. And we would usually find hanging on the back of the carriage two or three children from the other neighborhoods that he had passed through. They would sit quietly, and Hoppas could not see them from where he was sitting. We would scream at him:

"Turn it!"

Hoppas would turn suddenly the whip to hit the children who would then cower, lest they should catch a beating, and if they did, they wouldn't make a sound so as not to be betrayed.

"Turn it! Turn it!" we would continually urge Hoppas. "Harder. There are four!"

"Four?" Hoppas would get angry and would try to increase the range of the whip to reach the stowaways.

And we would scream "turn it" even when there were no children hanging on the carriage.

"Turn it! There are five!"

"Five?" Hoppas was outraged, and the whippings fell like rain.

Now that I write about Hoppas' "Turn it!" I remember also blind-Styllis. Even though he was blind from birth, he was an avid hunter.

"You will guide me and I will shoot," he said to the hunters who took him with them for fun.

He held the rifle up high and waited for the signal.

"On your right, Styllis."

Bam, bam! fired blind-Styllis.

"They are going left."

Bam, bam!

"Right again, Styllis."

Bam, bam!

"Did I catch anything?" he would ask.

"We see a feather falling. Let's check."

And they shouted even when there was nothing:

"They are on you, Styllis."

Bam, bam! fired blind-Styllis.

"Did I catch anything?"

The others roared with laughter.

Styllis' hunting was just for birds because it was dangerous to have the rifle turned to the ground for a rabbit. With today's space terminology, we would call it "surface-to-air hunting."

The story also contained a certain contempt for blindness. It resembled the contempt that I once witnessed surprised on a busy street in Bangkok: A young man about twenty years old was guiding a blind man the same age. They were chatting and joking and laughing. Suddenly the guide pushed the blind man urging him to cross the avenue at a dangerous spot pretending it was a sidewalk. He must have said in their language:

"This way."

The blind man was not fooled and stood firm.

"No way!"

He gave a little slap to his friend and they both burst out laughing. It was a real mockery of blindness in the middle of the road.

The children, on the other hand, who kept quiet at the whippings of Hoppas remind me, even though it's a little farfetched, of the two beggars, who, instead of competing, they decided to cooperate at the big fair of Apostolos Andreas.

"Whatever we get, we'll split it, okay?"

And of course neither of them was blind, as they both pretended to be.

So, at the splitting, one of them thinking that his partner was indeed blind, grabbed the money and ran and squatted quietly a little farther down.

"My Apostolos Andreas," the other one faked crying, "he stole what was rightfully mine. Do your miracle so that I can find him."

He took a rock, aimed and hit the "partner" on the back. The "partner" kept quiet. He ran on his tippy toes and sat somewhere else.

"My Apostolos Andreas, I can't find him," the "blind" man faked crying again. "Do your miracle now." He took a second rock, aimed and hit the "partner" who again did not say a word and sat somewhere else.

"My Apostolos Andreas, I can't find him," he cried loudly. "Do your miracle now on the third try."

He aimed and threw again. It was a hard rock and the "partner" jumped up:

"You can see, you stupid blind, you can see! You thought I would buy this nonsense about Apostolos Andreas and miracles! Come here. Let's split the money."

As for Hoppas, when the first cars appeared and everyone was circumspect about Hoppas' future, he himself was not.

"Even if airplanes come, Hoppas won't stop!"

And indeed he did not stop, even if gradually there was less business, his passengers left and he would take only a little cargo and an elderly friend. The carriage had also become a wreck and he had no money to fix it.

He would not admit his defeat.

"Old age beat me, not the cars."

So, we anxiously waited for Hoppas every evening to bring us news about mother's illness.

"What does it say about the injection, father?"

I was too young to understand that I was becoming the reason for my father to stay away from my mother during her final days, not to be at her bedside caressing her and giving her courage, the courage that no one but he could give her.

"Don't be afraid, Kalomoira."

It seems that one day they notified father that there was no hope. We returned to Skala in a rush without his telling me clearly the reason. We ran to mother's bedside. They had just combed her hair. They had also tied a blue ribbon on her hair. She looked at us sadly.

"You see what has become of me?" she said.

"What has become of you? You are just fine," answered father. "The way you always were."

"If Yiorgos saw me like this!" (She said it as if Yiorgos were the lover whom she should not disappoint).

"Stop now, Kalomoira," said father.

He bent down and kissed her. He leaned his face on hers for a long time.

We stayed two days, and they told me that I would go to Nicosia with my father.

To Nicosia? What was all this worry about me anyway? Because I was the only son who was left to preserve the family name? (Who planned the choice, who chose me for such responsibility?) And my father? Didn't they consider my father, didn't my father count? Would the "pale, shy girl" die without my father at her side holding her hand so that she would not be afraid? Did they have any idea how guilty I would feel when I understood? (No, don't say "they are children, they don't understand." They will understand one day, they will remember and understand one day and there will be no way to shake off the burden you loaded them with.)

They did not let me go near mother again (The family, mother. They say that the family must survive, they loaded me with it, mother, and they are making me a fugitive). I would see her from her bedroom door. And from the door I said goodbye to her:

"Adio, mama."

"Adio, my beloved son."

"I told Ayia Katerinoula" (I called her "Katerinoula" like the time of my measles, perhaps to remind of her power). "Don't be afraid."

Her eyes filled with tears.

"Really? I'm not afraid."

And mother died. They told me after they had buried her.

I made a dramatic interrogation to my sister who came to Nicosia to announce that to me.

"Are you saying that because there is no hope for her?"

"She died, I'm telling you."

Even the smallest distance from death, a small thread, would be enough for me.

"If she is dying tell me."

"She died, my Costakis."

She died? The word is engorged, it becomes huge, it fills the room.

Mother died? And what about me now?

"Don't say that she died of tuberculosis," recommended my sister. "Just say that she died of pneumonia."

"Why?"

"Because, first it was Yiorgos, and now mother; we will scare away the grooms."

She was right. When Irinia was getting married, her fiancé got an anonymous letter telling him what a sickly family we were.

"A family of consumption."

He read it to us and tore it up.

"Is it true that you were eating from Yiorgos' plate?" he asked Irinia.

"It's true."

"Bravo!" And (definitely, without having seen Shakespeare's "Twelfth Night") he hugged her.

I, however, did not forget my sister's advice. Girls might not want me either. And it is just now, and it is from this narration that my wife and my children and my friends will find out that my mother died, just like Yiorgos, of tuberculosis, that I was from a "family of consumption."

With mother's death, I perched like a frightened little bird in the love (what love!) of my one sister, Elengo, who had not got married yet, and my father. I would watch at night father's heavy breathing and get scared if for a moment I could not hear it.

"Father!"

He would wake up.

"Did you call me, my boy?"

"I had a bad dream," I would lie.

And there, what I was afraid of happened. Four years later (how did death choose the four-year intervals?) my father died too. Six months in bed with cancer.

And again, I was not supposed to get sad and not be able to preserve the family, and again, they were hiding it from me until the last minute, and I didn't know what pains were stabbing father. How can I pay up now, how can the family that I preserved pay up?

Suddenly I got the idea that someone in the house would die every four years. And even though things didn't happen exactly like that, when my two sisters—young, very young—died, again there was an interval of four years between the two deaths. And it was at a time when I was writing scripts for theater skits and in my grief I had a thought of black humor:

"Just like the Olympics then?"

I am risking another story here which I am not sure it would be appropriate to interpose.

After mother's death, we abandoned Skala.

"I threw a rock behind me," father would say.

We even wrote off our house. Who could face it again?

And there, forty years later, it was my luck to face it again.

I was supposed to go to Skala to see a friend on some business.

I called him and he gave me the address of his house: 26, Nikiforos Fokas Street. Where about was Nikiforos Fokas Street? When we lived in Skala, the streets had no names yet.

I took a taxi and the taxi let me outside my family house! I stood there staring in a daze. Should I leave, should I stay? The memories were enfolding me like a spider web. Here is the road of my childhood years. Two or three of the old houses were still there. The voices of the friends lived again. And our house! I hesitated a moment, two moments, and, as if hypnotized, I rang the bell. The door opened just as when I was coming home from school or from play. I went slowly up the stairs that I had gone down for the last time when I was twelve years old and mother was dying (Twelve years old? No, it was yesterday that I went down the stairs. Here I am going down scared and sorrowful, a step and a full stop, half a step and a full stop, a full stop and a black cloud).

"Do you know in which house you live?" I asked my friend.

How would he know? He was a stranger in town.

I told him. He felt sad.

"I'm sorry. How could I imagine."

I lived in another world. I went to mother's bedroom. Here was her bed. Strangely I was now seeking to sink as deeply as I could in my painful memories.

"Your mother came in too," said suddenly my friend, who was into spiritualism.

"What did you say?"

"I said that your mother came in too. Here she is. She is…."

And he described her to me, he described her pale foreign beauty, the structure of her face, her "bee-patterned" eyes.

I was at a loss. I was stunned like a little child.

"She is next to you and talking to you. She is saying, 'Did you finally come back, my beloved son?'"

"Don't!" I begged my friend. "Don't say anything else."

Then I changed my mind and I became mistrustful.

"Ask her what her name is."

"Even though I cannot get names, I'll ask her. She is saying something like 'Kallistheni.'"

"No, it wasn't Kallistheni. It was Kalomoira."

"They are similar," my friend rebutted without pity. "I said 'something like Kallistheni.'"

At night, when I returned to Nicosia, I could not sleep. I was home all alone (What do you mean "finally," mother? They would not let me come back, do you understand? The family had to be preserved). Logic could find no answer. I switched on all the lights and wandered around in all the rooms and the verandah. I went out to the street.

Nikos had no story. Jasmine has no story (even mother did not choose his leukemia to die of as she chose Yiorgos' tuberculosis. Even though she may have hesitated for a moment ["Can't I have both?"], she finally chose tuberculosis).

A little story of Nikos came up fifty years after his death, when we decided to put a new tombstone on our family grave in Skala. While we were discussing with the architect, the custodian of the cemetery approached us.

"Are you family?" he asked.

"Yes."

"I had a classmate Nikos Montis in elementary school."

"My brother."

"Your brother? Where is he?"

"In here," I replied, and showed him the grave.

"He died?"

"One of these bones is his" (One of these bones "cauterized" my mole on a Thursday afternoon).

The custodian became sad.

"When was he forgiven?" ("Forgiven? No, Nikos was not 'forgiven,' he forgave.")

"It's been a long time. Fifty years ago."

"Fifty years! Still a young boy?"

"Sixteen years old."

The custodian remained thoughtful.

"How come I hadn't found out about it? He had a heart of gold."

A month or so later, when I went again to Skala to see what happened with the grave, on the tombstone there was a single inscription:

"Family of Nikos Montis"

I asked neither the custodian nor the architect how the mistake was made. And I was not about to correct it either.

Time to go back to grandmother if I am going to salvage some coherence in my narration.

So, I was gathering her stories from all corners of memory, I was looking at them with a new look, I was studying them. Then I started researching. I chased names back to their roots, I chased incidents on the lips of old women and old men, I scrutinized historical and chronicle studies, archives, travel impressions in order to assemble afentis Batistas, who was tormenting me for so many years, to spread him out on paper so that I could finally find peace. It could not be, I was arguing, just four or five disconnected anecdotes without any pre–history or post–history.

And gradually a hinterland was becoming clear through the fog, more and more like the future in a crystal ball. And I could see now, I could see that the afentis was but the end of the string, that the fountainhead of the family was a different one, the fountainhead that grandmother did not know about so that she could narrate it to us and make our childlike eyes bulge four times more, bulge a thousand times more, make our chests swell to the point of bursting, and make a clean sweep of father's stories. And so, I started staying awake over the new fountainhead trying to reconstruct it, to find structure and texture, to sense the scenes and the dialogues.

Besides, I had the problem of what would happen to the other things that had preoccupied me earlier, what would happen to Batistas himself since someone else was becoming the main hero and Batistas was just his instrument, Batistas was just carrying out his orders and was pressuring me. Wouldn't it be an inadmissible decentralization? I did not know what to decide and the postpone-ments and the delays kept getting longer.

I asked the opinion of a friend of mine, and he helped me out. He said that that's how novels are written, that from being very far away and very broad, they start gradually getting narrower until they reach the focus of the lens. Hadn't I noticed that?

A novel, he told me, allows decentralizations so that it can get broader and embrace the periphery and become multipersonal and illuminate the interconnections of life. A novel is not a short story, which isolates and looks through a microscope. So, everything that I had written peripherally and circuitously could stay, and from this point on I had the freedom to digress and interpose as long as "I had Ithaca on my mind."

"Shouldn't, at least, the title change," I said, "if Ithaca is not Batistas?"

Useless question for I had already become so attached to the title that I could not change it. Besides, the "fountainhead" had no direct contact with me, it did not come to find me, I searched for it, it did not communicate orally by lips and ear, it came out of lifeless papers that if you read them, they are read, and if you do not read them, they stay there. The living thing, whose pulse had touched my feeling and my imagination, which was touching my bare skin through grandmother and my childhood years, which pulled up the cherries with it, was afentis Batistas. After all, it was afentis Batistas—I don't know with whose initiative, I don't know with whose slyness—that was watching me and urging me and pressur-ing me. So, I left the title "Afentis Batistas" and I simply added "and the other things." I admit that some of the "other things" were not as distant as the "fountainhead" nor did they come out of lifeless papers. On the contrary, they had a greater and more direct contact with me than afentis Batistas did, but, as I said, afentis Batistas was their cover however much it seems that I incidentally narrate them.

Under the pressure of afentis Batistas, I would start to write again and again and I would quit disappointed every time.

"No, I'm not a novelist. I cannot hold the end of the string and go so far away, I have no continuity, I get interrupted, I stop at the turns, I stop at the uphill roads of Lefkara."

Then I would start again.

"Why can't I do it, what's the meaning of I have no continuity? Everything is here, ready. Let's go."

"Let's go," but then I would quit again. On the third, fourth, fifth time I would close the manuscripts in another drawer; I would isolate them so that I would not see them, so that I would not tear them up. It was something like "protective custody," as we say in democracies.

However, the fact that I did not see the manuscripts did not help, because I would see Batistas himself. I would see him in my dream. I was surprised:

"Are you Batistas?"

"Yes."

"Afentis Batistas?"

"Yes."

"Grandmother used to say...."

"Forget about grandmother."

Forget about grandmother? How can I forget about grandmother?

He is suggesting that I look at him and readjust my memories to the new situation, readjust grandmother to the new data. And as if he had told me what to do, he is asking me if I am finished.

"Okay?"

And as if I knew, I replied:

"Okay."

"So, you were saying that you can't do it."

"Yes. I think I'm not a novelist."

He laughs.

"That's what Kazantzakis used to think."

"Who?"

"Nikos Kazantzakis."

Nikos Kazantzakis? That can't be right. How in the world did afentis Batistas know Kazantzakis?

He is suggesting that I look at him again so that I can convince myself that he really knew Kazantzakis. It did not matter that he preceded him, it did not matter at all however many years he preceded him.

I was completely under his control. He could tell me, and I would believe him, that he even knew Kazantzakis personally:

"We were classmates."

"Not classmates."

"Yes, classmates, I'm telling you."

"Where?"

"In high school; the Pancyprian Gymnasium of Heracleion."

"Yeah, right, the Pancyprian Gymnasium of Heracleion."

Every time, I don't know why, afentis Batistas would take on a different form. He would become an old friend, an old classmate, or someone I did not know. And neither was he always human. He could be a cat, a dog, and I knew by now for sure that it was afentis Batistas. I considered it completely redundant to ask who he was. Just superfluously and out of embarrassment I would confirm it:

"Afentis Batistas, right?"

"Yes. Your subject."

When he was silent, I could still hear him, from somewhere I could hear him:

"Sit down and write, apply yourself and write. Don't you see that you will barely make it? (However gently he tried to say it, the bottom line was that I would barely make it).

It was really a kind of neurosis, a delayed adolescent neurosis, even though it appeared only in the dark, even though it did not dare face the light of day. A nocturnal neurosis. Why not?

I even asked my friend the spiritualist from Skala, who, I knew, would not make fun of me.

"Write about him so that you can find some peace," he advised me. "There must be a reason that he insists."

"Write about him" was easier said than done. Because not "everything was ready," not "everything was here," as I had thought. Every little while someone had something to add, a friend from Famagusta who had heard something at home, a descendant of Katelia, grandmother's sister, or someone passing by the island, a Batistas from Corfu who, I don't know how and why, chose Cyprus to have his civil wedding with a rich American spinster. I was a godsend for him.

"We must be relatives," he told me.

And he used my connections with the District Officer and even made me a witness at his wedding. The District Officer gave me "congratulations," smiling knowingly.

"You just now met the groom?"

"Just now. It seems that my great-great-great-grandfather and his great-great-great-grandfather were relatives."

"Blood is thicker than water," smiled the District Officer.

He was reading somewhere, said the relative.

"Where?"

He cannot remember, unfortunately. It has been a long time. He will look for it and write to me.

They had a manuscript at home in Corfu, said the relative.

"And what did it say?"

He cannot remember, unfortunately. He will look for it and write to me.

"You won't forget?"

"Me? Forget? What are you talking about?"

What am I talking about? It seems that the "reading somewhere" and the "old manuscript" and all were only until he married the spinster, for I waited in vain for his letter. The only news I had was from the District Officer some time later.

"Your relative got a divorce."

"Which relative?"

"Your *koumbaros*. The great-great-great."

"Really?!"

The District Officer laughed.

"Either she figured him out quickly, or he spent all her money quickly."

With every new piece of information I would run back to my notes and correct and insert and revise ("I'm trying," I told the afentis, "you see how much I'm trying"). And indeed I was trying to restore the episodes, to separate the mixed-up passages and to glue together and make whole again the broken vessels, to look inside myself through them, to concentrate upon them, to perform percussion and auscultation.

And here I am finally, starting to write again, here I am finally, opening the closed manuscript drawer (I will barely make it).

The History textbooks talked about Frankish-occupied Ammo-chostos, Famagusta, with the powerful double walls, which Lala Mustafa besieged for a long time with his army and could not capture. And they talked about the Venetians, who protected it with bravery and perseverance, waiting for reinforcement, which was starting from Venice and stopping indecisive in Corfu and Souda and was finally leaving Souda and changing its mind in the middle of the sea and was going back.

The whole island had fallen into the hands of the Turks and nothing else was left to save the honor of Venice and Europe but the isolated and doomed castle of Kyrenia, and Famagusta.

The textbooks also talked about the heroic commander of the garrison of Famagusta, Antonio Bragadino, who repelled the raging Turkish attacks for months, until he realized the futility of the resistance when the reinforcement would not arrive, and he was forced to capitulate. They talked about the ferocious soldiers who entered the town and broke the treaty and slaughtered and dishon-ored and burned and ravaged. And Lala Mustafa, instead of sparing Bragadino's life, as he had agreed to do, flayed him alive.

With the fall of Famagusta, any Venetians who had survived scattered around the island and, in order to escape from the Turks, because it was primarily them that the Turks were chasing in the beginning, they pretended to be Greeks. And the Greeks, forbear-ing, put aside everything they had suffered from their rule and hid them and did not report them. Besides, they could see that now they had a common fate and a common enemy, the antichrist.

So the large and powerful family of the Batistases was scattered. They left their land and went far away into the interior of the island, so far away that the connection was lost, that the string was cut.

And the string was cut for my story too. For a hundred and thirty years, I could not trace the Batistases. They disappeared like a river under the pebbles. It was the period that the "relative" from Corfu gave me hopes of illuminating a little and which he did not illuminate. I kept thinking. Can a novel have such a gap? Is it right? Unless I left it open and threw in, like soil, anything else that might come along.

Just around 1700 start the stories about a Turkobatistas, who got his name from the friendships he had with the Turks. Was that perhaps another family, or was it the river popping out through the surface, popping out in such an unorthodox way, not at the mouth but high in Protochori of the Krasochoria of Troodos? If it was the same family, the story has some continuity. If not, you have two stories, two units, I don't know. In any case, a friend at the Center for Cultural Research disappointed me:

"You are creating a subject out of nothing. Turkobatistas was a different person. And did you have to bring that up now that the Turks have come back?"

The story goes that Turkobatistas had acquired so much power in the area that he did not mind revealing that he was Venetian and not Greek. And he would reveal it ungratefully and with the arrogance of the old masters of the island:

"Hey, I'm not Greek, do you hear me?"

At a moment of exaltation, he might even whisper:

"I don't worship, I'm not a slave!"

The Greeks were afraid of him and the agas of the district were trying to be in good terms with him, because he had traveled to Constantinople a few times and had managed to make some connections there, which, even though nobody knew exactly how important they were, just to be on the safe side, it was wise to be taken into account. Turkobatistas was implying them subtly:

"As I was saying, last year when I was in Constantinople...."

The pasha of the island was his friend, so he often received greetings and invitations from the Seraglio. Batistas, in turn, would give out lavish gifts and entertain the powerful people royally at the Krasochoria.

Therefore, the Greeks were justifiably afraid of him. They were afraid of him, but, at the same time, they owed him a lot. In their long and endless fights with other neighboring villages about the water, the grazing in the woods and other communal rights, the intervention of Turkobatistas always weighed a lot. In particular, the Krasochorians would mention how Turkobatistas had succeeded in their being allowed to open up underground tunnels and bring water from the other side of the mountain.

Only that it so happened that, in the same year, the running water of Klavia, a small Turkish village, was reduced. Klavia was the only Turkish village on Troodos. As a rule, the Turks would settle in the most fertile areas of the island, in the plains and the harbors, where it was also safer. Klavia was a strange exception. And the Klavians were fierce and "stabbers." Even if they were not Turks, even if they were not masters, the Krasochorians would still be afraid of them.

"I'll take you and leave you in Klavia!" people would scare the naughty children or tease the simpleton of the village.

And the simpleton would panic:

"Not in Klavia!"

A dramatic "Not in Klavia!" maybe the same as when, as children in Skala (I narrate this trying to lighten my conscience a little), we used to tease another simpleton, the German. It was the First World War, and it seems that the German was either fanatically on the side of the Allies or afraid that he might be accused of being a spy, so, when we called out to him "You are German," he would react with a woeful voice of protest:

"I'm not German! I'm not German!"

"You are, you are German!" we would continue without mercy.

He would become frantic and dangerous.

"I'm not German! I'm not German!"

When we could tell that he was ready to attack, we would run away shouting:

"You are German! You are German! You are, you are!"

The women would come out and enjoy the scene even if they pretended to scold us:

"Don't tease him. He'll have a stroke and it will be your fault."

And they would comfort him:

"Don't listen to them, you are British."

"British, British," the simpleton would say with relief, and in a voice like a deflating tire.

And since I mentioned the German, I also have to mention Patas, just to give a complete picture of childhood cruelty. Patas was a skinny, sweet, gentle, holy man, who could not step on a cross. Somehow we discovered his eccentricity, and, whenever we saw him, we would run before him and fill up the street quickly with crosses along its whole width. Patas was looking at them sorrowfully as if begging them to go away, and he would change direction. We would run again and fill the new street with crosses and then again the same until we would imprison the simpleton. The sadness was now imprinted on his face and he was begging us whimpering:

"Erase the crosses so that I can go home."

In the end we would condescendingly erase one cross.

"Come on, go through."

He would smile at us gratefully and struggle on his tippy toes to go through the narrow strip while we would guide him mockingly.

"You are doing great. A little more to the left. Don't rush. Slow down."

"There is a line," Patas would indicate to us.

"Just a moment and we'll erase it. Lift your foot. The other one too."

When he finally reached the other side, we would cheer and clap.

To this day, I feel a great deal of remorse about Patas. I can still hear his dramatic crying:

"Erase the crosses so that I can go home."

And while I am studying it, I wonder if there is something else to it.

"It sounds mystical," my spiritualist friend from Skala told me. "Who knows who Patas was and what karma he had."

However, my remorse about the German became less over the past few years, when the British and the Americans crucified the island and brought back the Turks (the same Turks and worse than during the first invasion four hundred years ago). I could imagine the German protesting now even more woefully:

"I'm not British! I'm not British!"

"You are American."

"I'm not American! I'm not American!"

Adapted to current events is today Lakis the "bomber." He always holds a little suitcase and goes around Ledra Street in Nicosia. His tease is "You put bombs."

"No, I don't put bombs!" screams the simpleton.

"You put bombs!" the accusation is repeated stronger here and there by youngsters and idle store owners. "You are a bomber! You are a bomber!"

And then Lakis opens his little suitcase and empties its contents on the sidewalk. A dirty towel, a sweater, a piece of bread, and a handful of olives scatter on the ground.

"Here! Look! Where are the bombs?"

All of them laugh. They laugh without realizing that now Lakis indeed put bombs, that it is bombs that he scattered on the sidewalk, bombs that cannot be disarmed by the police.

One day, as a joke, they secretly threw a ten-shilling bill among his things. He noticed it as he was picking them up and he put it aside.

"This is not mine."

"It was in the suitcase," they told him.

"No, it wasn't."

He closed his little suitcase and moved on.

"He was sure it was not his because it seems that he doesn't keep his money in the suitcase," said someone and laughed loudly.

The ten-shilling bill remained on the sidewalk awkward and exposed.

And farther down the same teasing:

"You put bombs."

"No, I don't put bombs. Ask the others who have seen my things."

"We don't ask anyone, we know. You are a bomber!"

Lakis is forced to open his little suitcase again, and again the dirty towel, the sweater, the bread, and the olives scatter on the sidewalk.

"Look. Where are the bombs?"

"What's this all about?" a British tourist passing by may ask.

It could be noted parenthetically here that simpletons are in general characterized by deep piety. They never miss church, always first in the morning mass, first in the evening mass, first in all the masses in their shiny shoes (the shining of the shoes has its own meaning). In fact, during the period that I am narrating, one of them, Vryonis, had kept order in the church of Galaktousa in Tersefanou. Even the church wardens could not keep such order. You could not utter a word during mass:

"Shhh, you down there!"

And neither then nor now would anyone be wrong to get enraged at the chatter of women in church; a chatter that introduced into the language of the common people the phrase "church talk," meaning "trivial, idle talk."

"I don't pay attention to such church talk."

"Can the issue be resolved with just church talk?"

(Since the phrase was created and is used by common people and not by skeptics, it must certainly have originated from the chatter of the church-going people and not from the liturgy books or the sermons from the pulpits).

There was only one time when Vryonis did not manage to keep order. Mrs. Myrianthi N. had come from Alexandria to meet her husband's relatives. She had brought along her little boy, Yiannis, four years old. It was Easter, and Mrs. Myrianthi went with her Yiannis to church, which was packed for the Easter Mass. In the crowd, Yiannis let go of her hand. Worried, Mrs. Myrianthi called out in a whisper:

"Yiannis!"

Vryonis did not spare her just because she was a visitor:

"Shhh!"

Mrs. Myrianthi was quiet for a few minutes and was looking through the gaps of people to see her Yiannis. When she could not see him, she called again a little louder:

"Yiannis!"

"Shhh!" Vryonis scolded her more intensely.

Mrs. Myrianthi threw a glance at him and quietly continued searching with her eyes. Then she defied him somehow and shouted for a third time in an increasing scale:

"Yiannis!"

"Shhh!" Vryonis was angry now.

Oh no, enough shhh. Mrs. Myrianthi did not care about the church or Vryonis anymore and shouted:

"With the 'shhh' of one and the 'shhh' of another, I'm not going to lose my Yiannis! Hey Yiannis!"

We had also heard about the "teacher" from Pano Pervolia. They called him "teacher" because he had studied for two years at the Seminary of Skala and stopped when he got sick with typhoid. He was fighting with death for three months. When he got well, he did not return to school. His nervous system had been shaken. There may have also been an underlying schizophrenic condition, which by chance presented itself during his illness. The villagers respected him and did not bother him. If they called him "teacher" it is because he liked it and wanted it too. So, the "teacher" would go to the funerals and his biggest worry was lest the priest should leave anything out. He knew the sermon by heart and would interrupt the priest angrily if he omitted something. He would scream:

"You skipped, my priest! For God's sake!"

Before the funeral started, they would warn the priest, just to be on the safe side:

"The 'teacher' is here too."

They would ask the "teacher" how come he did not correct the priest in other mysteries.

"Because we will hear those again," he would answer, "but the dead person will not hear the sermon of his funeral again."

And it was as if he timed the funeral. He looked at his watch like the Marathon runners.

"Slow down, my priest" ("Slow down, my priest, so that the dead person can follow. He is dead, poor man").

"Three quarters of an hour for a wedding, three quarters for a funeral too," he would say. "It's important for them to be the same, to be even. It's not by chance that they arranged them like this."

I mentioned that he interfered only in funerals. If he sometimes showed any interest in other mysteries, it was in jest or just to show that he was literate. At a wedding, for example, if the bride happened to be pregnant—very rare those days—he would whisper to the people around him:

"Did you hear that? The priest said it too. 'The virgin had a child in the womb.' It means that the baby is already cooking."

If they happened to comment that the priest did not say it of his own accord, but that it was written, he would reply:

"The people who wrote the sermons thought of everything. They probably thought that there may be such a case too."

The simpletons, however, (in spite of their piety, which can be easily explained) turn intensely against the divine when they believe that it's doing an injustice to them. Funny is the case of Hougias of Pyrogi. The simpleton would go late every afternoon to the chapel of Panagia Aimatousa and take half a shilling from the tray after he would first ask her humbly:

"May I take half a shilling, my Holy Mary, that I need?"

He would pick the coin discreetly with two fingers and leave walking backward and with continuous bows.

"Thank you, my Holy Mary. Until tomorrow."

After some time someone saw him and watched the process. He reported it to the Committee and the next day the sexton hid in the sanctuary behind the icon of Christ.

Having no idea about it, Hougias came at his usual time and asked his usual question:

"May I take half a shilling, my Holy Mary, that I need?"

"No!" said the sexton sternly.

Hougias was surprised, threw an angry glance at the icon of Christ from where the "no" had come and repeated his question:

"May I take half a shilling, my Holy Mary, that I need?"

"No!" said the sexton again more sternly.

The simpleton was flustered and turned angrily toward the icon of Christ:

"Tell me, why do You interfere? Who asked You? It's with Your Mother that I am talking. Is the money Yours? Just to spite You, I will get two half-shillings. Big deal!"

And I have to mention how wonderful he was when there was no money in the tray:

"They didn't give you even a little half-shilling today, my Holy Mary? Never mind, don't think about me. I'll get by. May I have your jasmine?"

He would take the jasmine from the icon and give the icon a loud, noisy, wide kiss just as he would give his mother. The Holy Mary must have appreciated that kiss a lot.

After the Turkish invasion of 1974, I saw some simpletons who were forced to abandon their villages and who concentrated in Nicosia. They looked lost. They would wander the unfamiliar streets and carry around such frustration that no other refugee carried around, a grief that I tried to turn into verses, but it could not concentrate and kept escaping me. If they met on the street people from their village, they would stop them and look at them sadly as if asking for an explanation. And if someone happened to tell them their old teasing, they would not reply. Only a smile like cry would bloom half a moment on their lips to confirm the memories that the teasing brought ("Now…").

In a realistic frame, after all, they had lost their old "supporters": the barber who would shave them free, the grocer who would give them a watermelon or a few cherries, the neighborhoods that would clothe them and feed them and make them coffee. They were literally "supporters," loyal "supporters" who had adopted them, so to speak:

"Have a seat, Loizos, and I'll get you something to eat. Have a seat, Loizos, to have a little coffee." (The diminutive implies that the coffee they were offering him was not a big deal, and not to be embarrassed about it.)

Contrary to the generous neighborhoods, the grocer was sometimes harsh:

"No cherries today, Loizos. No watermelon today, Loizos. Next week, when they are cheaper."

And Loizos was understanding. In fact, he would anticipate the grocer:

"No cherries yet, eh?"

With the difference that he would say it so often, that it would become pressing ("When finally?").

A merchant in Nicosia tried to help such a simpleton refugee:

"If I give you some transistor radios, will you manage to sell them?"

"Of course I'll manage."

And the merchant gave him, indeed, two or three transistor radios. And very early in the morning, at six o'clock, when the streets of the suburbs were filling up with peddling grocers, the voice of the simpleton could be heard too:

"Radios! Radios!" (Uttering "radios" with such entreaty, with such supplication, with such childlike supplication!)

"What is he selling at this hour?" wondered the surprised housewives, who came out sleepy and half naked.

"Radios!"

"Jesus Christ!"

Anyway, the Klavians protested, wrote letters, shouted, went to Nicosia. Nothing.

"It's not because of the tunnels," they were told, "that your water has been reduced. It's just a coincidence. We'll see."

"We'll see, we'll see," and they would not see. They left Nicosia and turned to the Krasochoria and threatened them:

"If you don't close down the tunnels...."

The Krasochorians were worried. Turkobatistas tried to calm them down:

"Don't worry about them. That's my business."

He always said "That's my business" with great pride, and he was enjoying it. "That's my business;" without explanation, closed and final. And the way it was closed like that, it inspired trust and confidence.

"Don't worry, Turkobatistas will take care of it."

And on a second, ungrateful level:

"The Frank knows what to do!"

The word "Frank" uttered with a certain remnant of an old inward aversion.

"The man is not a Frank," you might dare say.

"He is a Frank, he says so himself."

"He was once."

"He was and still is. Damn Frank!"

"I'll go and talk to them," said Turkobatistas.

The Krasochoria are surprised:

"In Klavia?"

"In Klavia."

The Krasochoria are afraid lest he should ask for another couple of people to go with him and are relieved when Batistas tells them that he will go alone. He knew the Krasochorians and said that that was the way it should be done.

"In such cases if you can't go alone, don't go at all. It cannot be done otherwise, it doesn't work."

And the Krasochorians, again on a second, ungrateful level:

"If he didn't have any friendships with the Turks, I doubt that he would have the guts."

And Turkobatistas went to Klavia. He went riding on his tall mule with the white saddle and the embroidery from Fyti with the blue beads on the forehead. It was the new mule, which he got when the bishop came one day to the village on a taller and more beautiful mule than the one that Turkobatistas had at the time. He was piqued when he saw people admire her, and he sent his people to look in the plains for a better one. And he found one. He paid well, and he found one.

"I'll even change the adage," he would say laughing. "Don't say anymore 'would that the bishop's mule kicked you,' but rather 'would that Batistas' mule kicked you!' If nothing else, it's not appropriate for the bishop's mule to kick people! This way I'm saving the bishop too. Let Batistas' mule kick as much as she wants, she has every right, she holds no high office, she's a commoner; whenever she feels like it, she kicks!"

As Turkobatistas was entering Klavia, the guard dogs barked at him threateningly and the men looked at him fiercely with threats and curiosity.

So this was Turkobatistas they had heard about? *Buçuk* Turk? Where?

He calmly crossed the village. The mayor of the village and the council members received him and treated him coldly. The other Klavians gathered also at the coffeehouse, and Turkobatistas talked to them.

He told them that he was coming as a friend. The Krasochorians were sending their regards and the message not to worry, because, if it becomes clear that the tunnels indeed affected the running water of the village, they will close them down.

They listened to him suspiciously.

"The thing is clear," said one of them.

"No, it's not clear," replied Turkobatistas. "The second August will determine that."

The Klavians did not wait for the second August. Not many days had passed and they "blocked" some tunnels. The Krasochorians patiently opened them up; the Turks blocked them again. A shepherd was even found stabbed to death. The Krasochoria fired up:

"Stabbers or not…."

Turkobatistas was holding them back.

"We can't, my friends. We are not strong enough. Let's not go to extremes. However you look at it, it's a Turkish village. Does the nail separate from the finger? Leave it to me; that's my business."

And it was indeed his business. The police went to Klavia for interrogation, a penalty was imposed to the village to rebuild the tunnels, the mayor and the council members were warned, and the Klavians did not do any more harm.

Time passed and the second August came to "determine." The second August was neither a Greek nor a Turk and gave a fair trial. Klavia's running water was dangerously reduced, and Turkobatistas said to the Krasochorians:

"We are closing down the tunnels!"

"What is the Frank talking about?"

The Krasochorians revolted.

They said no, they shouted. *Aman, zaman.* Turkobatistas was unshaken.

"We are closing down the tunnels. That's final."

And the tunnels closed down, and the Klavians could not believe their eyes:

"*Nasıl adamdır!*"

Besides, in their most difficult personal moments, when they did not know what to do, the Krasochorians went to Turkobatistas.

"I'll go to the Frank!"

Not even now could the second, ungrateful level be spared.

Batistas never refused to help. He would give them money and even save them from jail as long as he knew that he had hopes of succeeding, because he was very careful not to let his interventions fall off. Therefore, the Greeks were wondering.

"What kind of a man is he anyway?"

And indeed, what was he, what game was he playing, what purpose did he have?

Game or not, one day everybody started sensing that for the past few months something was wrong. Turkobatistas would not leave the estate, the trips to Nicosia stopped, and Turkish guests had not been to Protochori in a very long time. Besides, however willing Batistas was before to help so much he now refused without even waiting to hear about the problem.

"It cannot be done!"

"It serves us right," the Krasochorians were saying at the beginning. "On every occasion we used to consider him a Frank."

Soon, however, they suspected that other were the reasons for the change of Batistas and for the first time they realized what "the Frank" was for the area. They started worrying.

"Three times in a month came his parents-in-law from Limassol. And everybody at the estate had a long face."

One day Turkobatistas left for Nicosia. It seems that indeed something serious was going on and that he decided finally to face it. He knew well that, even if the pasha had stopped his contacts with him, he could still rely on his friendship.

Batistas stayed for two weeks in Nicosia. And the Krasochoria could not find peace. They had no other topic of discussion.

"Is he back?"

"No."

"That's strange."

"Doesn't kokona-Maria know?"

"She doesn't say."

"He is gone, the Turks bumped him off."

No, the Turks did not bump Batistas off. He returned to the estate. And again the in-laws came from Limassol and again the long faces at the estate. And one day the news that Turkobatistas was changing religion dropped like a bomb. The Krasochoria were shaken.

"It was all pretense, everything was planned in advance," said some people.

"He is a Frank, what did you expect? Frankishness is in the blood."

"And he was saying that he was not a slave, that he did not worship God. Now he is saying a thousand prayers to Allah!"

The proselytism ceremony took place at the old catholic cathedral of Ayia Sophia in Nicosia, which, after the capture of the island, had been turned into a mosque. Incidentally, it is worth noting here that the Turks turned only the catholic churches of the island into mosques. It seems that they realized that this way they were not insulting the local orthodox population, which had suffered from the Catholic Church.

Both the Franks and their churches are foreign, they thought. Their reign is over.

And two minarets would be attached to the sides of the cathedral to confirm the end.

Perhaps, however, they were not even interested in the orthodox churches, because structurally they were unremarkable and there could be no comparison whatsoever with the majestic catholic cathedrals of Nicosia and Famagusta, which took many decades to be built and especially to be made so majestic, because they were intruders and foreigners and defending a lost case.

Anyway, the proselytism ceremony of Turkobatistas took place at Ayia Sophia. And at his mansion in Protochori, the event was celebrated for a whole week.

The villagers were trying as much as they could to stay away from the celebrations even if they were careful with their words.

"Where is your son? Isn't he coming?"

"Why wouldn't he come, afentis? Work is keeping him."

"What work? Couldn't he spare a moment?"

"He will come, afentis."

"I don't care, tell him. Tell him not to come."

The old nanny who had raised Turkobatistas had not gone to the celebrations either. She went a few days later.

"Where were you, old woman?"

"I was sick, son. Old age."

She sat near him. She looked at him without speaking. Tears were filling her eyes slowly so as not to be perceived.

"Why are you doing this, old woman? I'm not leaving."

"Yes, you are, son," dared bitterly the nanny.

He held her head, caressed her, and talked to her gently:

"It's not your business to be searching this, old woman. Give me your blessing."

The Krasochorians were, in general, moving discreetly away from Turkobatistas. He saw that and did not care:

"Who pays any attention to them anyway?"

Batistas' conversion caused a stir in the Krasochoria. They were afraid that he might not stand by them like before, that he might become one with the Turks. And then the idea was thrown for papa-Vasilis to go and see him, chat with him, fish for information, advise him. You never know....

Papa-Vasilis was the priest of Protochori, and although the Krasochoria had other priests too, he was the main representative of God in the area since Protochori was its center. The other churches were like branch stores and their priests like branch store owners. Papa-Vasilis liked the recognition, and he accepted and promoted it. How could he ever imagine that one day he would regret it?

It was also his duty to go, they said. He should have thought of it himself. A sheep has wandered off from the flock and has been led astray. Won't the shepherd run after it?

"It's not the same, my good people," said faint-heartedly the simple priest. "Turkobatistas is not a sheep."

"Same or not, sheep or no sheep, you just have to go and talk to him, my priest."

"And tell him what? Can such things be undone? Now I play, now I don't? It's not a 'lingri' game."

Papa-Vasilis was mostly afraid lest his action should reach the ears of the Turks.

"You'll have God with you, my priest," they urged him.

It was the first time that the mention of God did not shake his doubts and hesitations. He passed it by and tried another argument:

"I don't want to have the villages on my conscience."

And he enforced and narrowed down his argument:

"I don't want to have you on my conscience either."

Nothing. The Krasochorians were not convinced and the pressure continued.

"Search your conscience, my priest."

"It's my conscience that I'm searching, people."

The pressure was great. Some old women started in fact having "visions" of the Holy Mary. Even the priest's wife considered it her ultimate religious duty to pressure him.

"You must go, my priest."

Papa-Vasilis looked at her surprised ("Even you, wife?").

It was the first time that she talked back to him, the first time that she discussed his views, which until now were axioms for her (The respect that the priests' wives in the villages feel for their priests is indeed curious. As if they got married to a saint, as if they were given the favor of marrying a flawless saint.

"My priest—'my,' a huge, proud 'my'—says that…").

114

Under so much pressure and when he saw his wife jump into the other camp, papa-Vasilis surrendered like Caesar.

"Okay, I'll go tomorrow."

The news traveled like lightning.

"Tomorrow the priest will go to Turkobatistas!"

"I'll go up to the church of the Savior in the afternoon to light his lamp," said his wife touched.

The priest paid no attention. The Savior and the lamp meant nothing to him today. His mind was fixed on the "slaughter of the patriarch" as he had heard it from the head priest at Koidani.

The next day he said goodbye to his wife and children as if he were going on a trip.

"Why are you acting like this, my priest?" asked his wife. "For God's sake!"

Papa-Vasilis left without answering.

Several people accompanied him up to the boundaries of the estate and let him go. They let him go just as you let a kite go. With the difference that papa-Vasilis did not fly like a kite, he crawled slowly and hesitantly. And the people were almost making fun of him.

"Look how he is walking! As if being led to the gallows!"

Reaching the door of the mansion, papa-Vasilis turned to the crowd and waved his hand as if to take courage or to say goodbye:

"I'm going. Forgive me and God forgive you!"

Turkobatistas welcomed him. He showed some surprise.

"Welcome, my priest!"

He offered him dessert and coffee. They talked about the weather, the crop, this and that.

"How is kokona-Maria?"

"She is fine. Shall I call her?"

"No, no, don't bother her. How is Antonellos?"

"Just fine."

"I see him in the village. A handsome and upstanding boy. Congratulations."

Then they ran out of subjects and they both remained quiet.

In order to break the silence and, at the same time, postpone the moment of trial a little longer, papa-Vasilis said:

"The time must be either twenty to or twenty after."

Turkobatistas took out of his vest his big silver pocket watch with the ornamented lid and the Arabic inscription.

"Yes, it's twenty after nine. How did you know?"

Papa-Vasilis explained to him that when the conversation suddenly stops, it means that an angel is passing by. The mind goes blank, the tongue is tied. And he always passes by at twenty to or twenty after.

"Really? I didn't know that. What's with the twenty minutes?"

"I don't know, perhaps it's the time that it takes him to go up or down."

New silence.

"The 'twenty after' has passed, and we are silent again," said Turkobatistas.

"Yes," whispered papa-Vasilis.

"You wanted to tell me something," Turkobatistas helped him. "Speak freely, don't worry."

"It was my duty, you know, sior Batistas. Do you understand?"

"I understand," said Turkobatistas.

A small pause.

"You understand," repeated papa-Vasilis.

"I understand," said again Turkobatistas.

Another small pause as if the angel were going back and forth playing with them and the clock, like an accomplice, going now forward, now backward showing "twenty after" or "twenty to."

"Listen, my priest," said Turkobatistas. "Tell them that you talked to me. You won't be lying. You talked to me in your own way, which is probably the best."

"When a sheep," stuttered papa-Vasilis.

"I know. Tell them that I'm not a sheep. Tell them that I didn't do it out of foolishness so that I can correct it."

He went to the window and looked out.

Papa-Vasilis took courage. If he could at least tell him why he did it, he would have something to convey back. Unfortunately, Turkobatistas bypassed the immediate continuation of the conversation and said obliquely and looking constantly out of the window as if he were talking to someone out in the grove:

"What's the use? God is one, my priest, one, and the people are many. He has no problems, we have the problems, and He gave us the brains to solve them."

Papa-Vasilis did not show that he agreed. In fact he wanted to tell him:

"What are you saying? That He gave us brains so that we could become Turks?"

He did not say that, and Turkobatistas was able to change the subject. And he did.

Papa-Vasilis realized that the subject was closed. He caressed his beard nervously.

"That's all."

He got up to leave. Turkobatistas did not stop him. He escorted him outside.

"Thank you, my priest, for coming. Go in good health."

And papa-Vasilis left. The villagers, who were impatiently waiting for him, saw him walk back as crawlingly as he had gone.

"Well?"

He delays a little to answer.

"Nothing."

"What nothing?"

Nothing. He had told them so. Can such things be undone? The Turks should not find out about it. He is not a sheep, he said. God is one, he said.

"And what did you answer?" asked sternly an educated one.

"What could I answer? Is it easy to answer? I didn't know what to say."

The educated one scrunched his eyebrows.

"You didn't know? You should have told him you agree that God is one, but what about the mediators? Don't the mediators count? The mediators are the important ones. God listens only to the mediators. Will He sit and listen to each one of us separately? Does He have time to listen to each one of us separately? I have my representatives, gentlemen, He says; talk to them. There are not just five or ten or a hundred or a thousand of you. There are millions of you, I cannot do everything."

Papa-Vasilis was listening carefully.

"You are right, I didn't think of that," he said apologetically and humbled. "It's not that I was scared to talk."

The educated one did not say "Of course you were scared," perhaps because he preferred for the priest to be proven ignorant and unskillful rather than simply a coward.

And the people—who do not need much of an excuse to start gossiping—slandered papa-Vasilis biliously.

"I really believe that he didn't mention a thing to him. He drank his coffee in peace and left. As if he had gone to congratulate him on his change of faith."

And it was a good opportunity for some to remember some other incident with papa-Vasilis. That, for instance, it was a lie that he, like the God-fearing priests, never took a bath lest the holy myrrh of priesthood should get washed away.

"He goes secretly to the river and takes a bath, I'm telling you. I saw him one day at early dawn from Pentanemo. As naked as the day he was born. You should see how he was enjoying the water! What somersaults!"

"Are you sure it was papa-Vasilis?"

"What do you mean am I sure? Does anyone else have a beard?"

"Why don't we ask his wife?" joked another one. "She is the only one who must know for sure!"

Even the priest's wife doubted that her priest talked to Batistas. And she took advantage of a single tender moment to ask him.

"I said that I talked to him," the priest was agitated, and the tender moment was lost, the tender moment that came so rarely anymore, which was not like before when only Sundays and holidays could control it.

(The priests are very careful and they put big warning crosses in front of every holiday on their calendars. And of course there are jokes about some priests' wives who erase some crosses or, on an unbearable night, they hide the calendars altogether.

"Is the calendar okay, wife?"

"It's okay, trust me, my priest."

To the observance of holidays many people attribute the fact that by a strange coincidence the priests' daughters are so beautiful.

"They are begotten with God's blessing and with sacrifices, not with dirt!"

When the calendar was found again, the priest's wife would confess:

"Temptation, my priest; Satan wanted to befoul us!"

"You should conquer him, wife, you should conquer him!"

He would then impose on her a few genuflections, a little bit of fasting, a few prayers and that was it.)

The priest's wife did not consider the loss of the tender moment and she insisted:

"What did you tell him?"

"What did I tell him…what did I tell him…he understood. He is not some little woman who needs a lot of talk. It's a sin that you don't believe me, wife. I won't let you receive the Holy Communion on Sunday!"

The truth is that papa-Vasilis got a lot of headaches with Batistas' conversion. On the one hand, the Krasochorians considered the dealing with the situation his responsibility, on the other hand, an unforeseen competition started, a competition that had to do with him specifically, and that the Krasochorians did not let the peace-loving priest ignore, much as he would like to.

The competition was coming from the hodja. As far back as the Krasochorians could remember, a hodja had never set foot in their villages. He set foot for the first time one morning after Turkobatistas' proselytism. He crossed Protochori proudly on his mule heading for the estate. The people went to the doors and hung on the windows to look at him as if he were a strange phenomenon.

"A hodja!"

They ran to notify papa-Vasilis as if asking him to save them. They announced it the same way they would announce "Fire!"

"Papa-Vasilis, a hodja!"

Papa-Vasilis went out indolently. Jesus Christ! A new headache now!

"Okay, people," he said. "Why are you getting upset? Be calm! It's not the end of the world. It's just a hodja. In Nicosia the hodjas go back and forth, day and night, and nobody even turns to look at them."

They listened to him with pity.

"Listen to that!" (It was definitely the priest who was bathing stark naked in the river!)

All day the village had no other topic.

"Here are the consequences. God have mercy on us."

In vain did they wait until the afternoon to see the hodja leave so that they could have a better look at him. The hodja spent the night at the estate and left the next day. He left as triumphantly as he had come, with the people at the doors and windows staring. They even notified papa-Vasilis:

"The hodja is leaving!"

"Let him go in good health," said the priest stoically (He almost said: with God's blessing). "Is that all we will worry about now, he is coming, he is leaving?"

"Yes, we'll worry about him, my priest. Is that a small worry?"

They would get angry:

"Jesus Christ! He couldn't care less!"

As the hodja was approaching, the children would hide frightened behind their mothers and clutch at their clothes.

Perhaps they had heard about the hodjas what we, as children, would hear about the Jews:

"Now that the Jew will pass by, I will let him suck your blood!"

It was probably a long subconscious memory of the big massacre that the Jews had done on the island, a memory which we carried with us from grandfather to grandfather and was terrifying us (and which only recently, when we started having tourists from Israel, did we try to fight and ignore the massacre too). We would not even ask who the Jew was and why he would suck our blood. We knew by birth. And we knew that he passed often by our narrow street as soon as night fell, just like the yogurt seller or the peanut seller. We could even describe him to you. And if you want to know, the sulky old man had blood in his flask, not vinegar as he was proclaiming. Did you see how wickedly he was looking?

The hodja's visits, however sparse, were a great ordeal for the Krasochoria. Even though a hodja was quite common in the towns and villages of the plains, in the remote mountain area of the Krasochoria, the way he was so novel, they regarded him as a Turkish bridgehead and a dangerous wedge. They even said:

"As if it were not enough to worry lest we should see the priest early in the morning, now we will also worry lest we should see the hodja!"

They were afraid as much of meeting a priest early in the morning as of, maybe even more, running into him on a remote road or in a grove, where there were no others to share the bad luck, and the whole thing fell on you.

"If it's one time bad luck with the priest, it's ten times with the hodja!"

The bad luck of an "early morning" meeting with a priest was and still is a strong superstition both in the villages and in the towns.

"What happened to you today? Did you see a priest early in the morning?"

The most effective antidote for such an "early morning" encounter is an obscene gesture.

Even worse than the "early morning" of the priest is meeting in the street or seeing early in the morning someone who has the evil eye. In this case, the obscene gesture cannot help, the incense cannot help, there is no antidote. In the villages, where people know each other, there are such branded people. The reputation of some even goes beyond the boundaries of their village, as in the case of Koutsopantelis from the Kokkinochoria. If the villagers happened to run into him on their way to work, they would go back.

"Why did you come back?" asked their wives.

"I ran into Koutsopantelis."

They justify their superstition with the fact that supposedly also the Holy Mary feared the "evil eye." The story goes that someone had given her the evil eye, and that her head hurt, and that in order for her to get well, Jesus ordered incense with olive tree leaves.

For papa-Vasilis, the visits of the hodja became a nightmare. Everybody was looking at him as if asking him what will happen finally.

And the ordeal reached its peak when the devil brought it about one day so that papa-Vasilis and the hodja ran into each other.

"Go behind me, Satan," whispered papa-Vasilis when he saw the hodja at the turn of the road.

Unfortunately, it was too late for Satan to go behind him (and why should he, anyway?) or for himself to reverse and avoid the meeting.

Papa-Vasilis realized that it was not a mere meeting, it was a clash. Only that he did not think of it as a clash between Christ and Mohammed, and he dealt with it on its low realistic level as a clash between two ordinary people one of whom was the master of the island and the other the slave, a clash that required a lot of caution. So he thought it prudent to bow with respect. The hodja replied arrogantly to the greeting and passed without stopping.

Papa-Vasilis stayed still for a while looking at the hodja, who was walking away. He felt insulted and humiliated.

"Bad meeting early in the morning," he said.

It was on the tip of his tongue to say "ptu ptu thirteen" and for a moment he thought of making, for the first time in his life, the obscene gesture that neutralizes the meeting with a priest (I forgot to say that the priests know about this gesture, they know that as soon as they pass, people will make it, and they don't care. After all, they know that people do not mean it, that it comes automatically and unwittingly).

Papa-Vasilis avoided the temptation of the gesture and continued on his way, and the episode would be over, but as his bad luck would have it, some people witnessed the scene and made him curse the day he was born.

"Do you know what you did, my priest?"

"What did I do?"

"You bowed Christ in front of Mohammed. That's what you did."

"No, my good people. I did not bow Christ. It's papa-Vasilis that I bowed. Leave Christ alone. Don't sin."

"And who is in Christ's place in the village?"

Papa-Vasilis did not know what to reply. After this went on for a while, he got mad:

"Listen. I acted according to my conscience and as my little brain instructed me. If you think that I shamed Christ, take the cassock and look for another priest!"

The hodja had little regard of his victory over papa-Vasilis. He was just a small, insignificant priest, a foot path. He wanted the bishop. He wanted the two of them to meet on their mules like roosters or like knights who would fight with spears, and to have people gather around and watch. Then it would really be worth it.

"I got into your boundaries, my bishop!"

The possibility of such a meeting was also being discussed in the village with the hope that the humiliation of Christ by Mohammed would be washed away, and that they would take back Christ's blood.

They said to papa-Vasilis:

"If it had been the bishop, is that what he would have done?"

"I don't know what the bishop would have done. I'm not a bishop. I'm a priest, a plain priest, a nutshell, a fly."

And he wanted to tell them that the patriarch was a bishop, and in fact, not just a bishop, but a bishop of bishops and still they eliminated him.

Anyway, the fact is that papa-Vasilis had lost the respect of his people, and either to show him that or to stop another "humiliation" of Christ, every time they saw the hodja coming, they would run to notify him as if telling him "Hide!" And papa-Vasilis would become a wreck.

The bishop, on the other hand, by some weird coincidence, never met with the hodja in Protochori. After a while some people suspected that papa-Vasilis was notifying him.

"It seems that he doesn't want us to see the difference, it seems that he wants us to believe that the bishop would probably do the same if he were in his place."

Nevertheless, most people did not agree.

"Let's not overdo it, people. How can he possibly know when the hodja is coming so that he can notify the bishop? We have to say what's right."

"Unless...," said someone.

"Unless what?"

"I don't know, maybe Turkobatistas himself notifies him."

Turkobatistas? Was that possible?

"Everything is possible with the 'linobambakos.'"

The characterization was wrong. "Linobambakos" meant something else. There were a few thousand people in the area of Louroutzina near Skala and in the valley of Solea who, even though they were Turks, spoke Greek and had secretly holy icons in their houses and they lit lamps and went to the fair of Ayios Georgios Kontos and of the Cross and mingled with the crowd and worshipped unnoticed. Who knows from what failed levy of children their history started, from what remainder of Greeks of Asia Minor, from what untamed remnant of isolated Pontians or Laz. People called them "linobambaki," meaning impure, neither linen nor cotton. And it was with regard to them that the Church made the historic and one of its biggest mistakes to refuse to baptize them Christians during the British occupation when they took courage and asked for it.

"I don't want dogs in my flock!" the archbishop had said.

So fifty years later, this mistake too was paid dearly.

It was the fatal destructive mentality that held back the Greek progressive majority from the small and underdeveloped Turkish minority and prohibited the assimilation, and the result was that the two communities remained a prey to foreign propagandas and were incited to mutual destruction.

As bad luck would have it, it was a year of terrible drought. September, October, November went by without a drop of rain. The sky was shining blue, without a trace of cloud. December came and still no rain. The weather was fine. It was still summer on the name days of Ayios Nikolaos and Ayia Varvara, when normally "the walls shake." The people were terrified.

"God will waste us."

Since there was no snow at all on Troodos, the water level dropped and the springs started drying up one after the other as if being in line; even "Chrysovrysi," which had never dried up. None of the old people remembered such a drought. In vain did they pray, in vain did they circle the church with double, triple rope (What meaning this had—and still has—I don't know. Is it maybe black-mail? "There, until you rain!"), in vain did the villagers go crawling up to the chapels of Prophet Elias on the mountain sides (on the mountain sides so that his grace will be halfway to God and he can convey more easily, on the mountain sides so that he can rule from up there over the storms and the lightnings, just as we painted him).

Someone said:

"We come up here only when we need him. How do we expect him to listen to us?"

"This high up where he lives, great be his name...."

(Great be his name, but the Turkish invasion of 1974 took place by weird coincidence on July 20, his name day.

"On such a day? What a nerve!" commented some people.

"Maybe they didn't know it was his name day," said sarcastically a leftist intellectual.

"Zeus would be better, I'm telling you," said another. "He would hurl his lightning bolts!"

Someone defended Prophet Elias:

"Let's not blame everything on the prophet! Did Apostolos Andreas cut down a Turkish hand as he had done in the old days when a Turk tried to light his cigarette from his lamp? With the way the world has become, the saints have their instructions too. In this day and age, it's a tough job to be a saint."

And about Zeus, one could easily reply that he was Greek, whereas today we do not have anyone of ours in heaven. Neither God is Greek nor Jesus nor anyone of the powerful ones, even if we say that a saint is protecting our canons and another saint our infantry and another one our navy).

The fear of drought was (and still is) for the island like the fear of an unavoidable earthquake or the fear of cholera.

"It doesn't even drizzle this year," they would despair.

They would go back to the old days, when there was a drought for seventeen years straight, and the people left and went to Constantinople, and the place was filled with snakes and Ayia Eleni brought cats—"Cavo Gato" was called the promontory where she unloaded them—to eat them.

(About the cats of the island, it would be worth interposing here that, to this day, many people in the villages believe that we have borrowed them, that they still belong to Ayia Eleni and not to us. This notion was reinforced—and the newspapers wrote about it too—in the Second World War, when a caique, loaded with cats to take to Libya to eliminate the desert snakes, which were threatening the British army, sank as soon as it was out of Cyprus waters, and the cats drowned.

"Did we ask first Ayia Eleni if she agrees?" some people said half jokingly. "She may be a Germanophile!")

Many people even knew what the "prophetic" books and the books of the saints said about the future droughts (and it is strange that they memorized so faithfully a language that they did not understand very well):

"For three consecutive years the island will have no rain from the sky and there will be great hunger and screams of anguish."

"What does 'Agathangelos' say?" they were looking for a more valid opinion.

Even though probably nobody had read "Agathangelos," in order to be more convincing, people used to attribute everything to him.

"'Agathangelos' says...."

And that took no dispute.

"He doesn't talk about droughts," said the intellectual one. "He talks about wars and other disasters."

The answer implied that droughts were not a specialty of "Agathangelos," or that, at least, they were not among his interests.

What about the Apocalypse of John?

"What do you tell him now?"

The droughts were more significant to the island as a whole when they struck the mountains rather than the plains, because the mountains were the ones receiving the main bulk of the precipitation in order for the underground waters to be enriched and for the rivers, the Pedieos and the Serrachis, to start flowing toward the plains of Mesaoria and Morphou.

It was, therefore, natural for everyone to seek the reason of the threatening relapse of God's old wrath.

For the Krasochorians, the reason was first of all (they said it out of habit without deep down believing it) their "sins" ("Specifically which sins?" "In general" [The expression "in general" is harmless]) and then Batistas' conversion.

"You think God will take Batistas into account, my friends?" disagreed Papa-Vasilis, who could see where they were headed.

"Of course He will take him into account, why wouldn't He? However you look at it, He gets annoyed and becomes stubborn. And it's also the issue of setting an example for the others. He thinks, 'let me punish the offense now that it's still the beginning.'"

In strengthening the suspicions of the Krasochorians, some old women started again having dreams of the Holy Mary telling them that all the disaster stemmed from Batistas' change of faith.

The matter was very serious. They were forced to venture very faint-heartedly to give some hints to Turkobatistas.

"We are not going to have any rain this year, sior Batistas. What do you think?"

And then:

"It seems that our sins have gotten heavier."

However much they did not dare tell him yet about the old women's dreams, they would no doubt tell him if the drought continued. They were planning the announcement and were looking at papa-Vasilis meaningfully. Should they send him again, should they not? Papa-Vasilis was reading this in their look and was shrinking and waiting stoically for the sentence ("Whatever God wants").

And one day the priest's wife said that she also saw the Holy Mary in her dream. The priest got angry.

"I'm not buying these tricks, wife. You became one with the senile old women? As if the Holy Mary had nothing else to worry about!"

He even used an old argument of the intellectual's:

"If God had something to announce to us, He has His representative in the village, who, after all, understands what he is told!"

Anyway, nobody knows how the situation would have developed if pelting rains and storms and heavy snow had not suddenly started at the end of December. So, the people forgot immediately about their "sins" and Batistas' conversion and the dreams of the old women, and they freed the churches from the rope wallcuffs ("Okay, you are free now, you may continue with your Christ"), held doxologies with cheerful, chirping bells, opened the "pots" with the "corned meats," took down the ham and the "strings" of sausages, and sat day and night at the "hearth" eating and drinking to the song of the rain and the wind.

The villagers said to papa-Vasilis as if he knew what they were thinking and what they were planning:

"It didn't come to that."

"Thanks a lot," replied papa-Vasilis.

One way or another the villages understood what a dangerous wedge Batistas' change of faith was.

"You will see that slowly he will even build a small mosque at the estate with its little minaret, with its everything, and one fine morning we will suddenly hear the muezzin. And he will be right. He cannot leave his business and go miles away from the village to pray.

"Troubles that came to us out of the blue!"

They thought of Peristerona, on the way to Nicosia, which had a church and a mosque across from each other, just a few steps apart. They would see them and cross themselves.

"How can these people attend mass? With what heart can you pray and hear the hodja of the Turks? And how does God tolerate this?"

"God doesn't mind probably because He does not hear what the hodja is saying. His prayers cannot reach His ears."

As a matter of fact, Turkobatistas used to go about once a month to the mosque in Limassol, and sometimes, even though it was farther away, to Nicosia so that the Seraglio would find out about it too.

And whenever the Krasochorians saw him in his Victoria carriage all dressed up and wearing his new fez, they would say:

"At least we have also Mohammed watching over us...."

And they would whisper sarcastically:

"*Güle, güle!*"

As for the fear lest a mosque should sprout and even the hodja's visits (is it necessary for him to come here, can't there be any other arrangement?) they agreed that they had to talk to Turkobatistas.

"What can we do, it was not needed during the drought, my priest…."

"Thanks a lot," said again papa-Vasilis interrupting them.

"Unfortunately now you have to go. You understand how serious the matter is."

Papa-Vasilis decided to decline the main representation of God in the Krasochoria.

"The Krasochoria have other priests too."

"Really? All this time they didn't have any. Now you remembered them?"

And besides how did he expect other shepherds to be running after his own sheep? Run, because I'm afraid?

"The sheep belongs to all," noted papa-Vasilis, "it doesn't have the seal of Protochori on its butt!"

He tried something else too. Wouldn't it be better if the bishop went?

"We cannot ask the bishop to risk it," they answered.

"That's true," said papa-Vasilis, "we must not put the bishop in danger. While what is one priest more, one priest less, it doesn't matter. Right?"

Something like that.

"We have fallen very low, people," summarized papa-Vasilis bitterly. "Today we don't look at the patriarch, we look at his deacon, the deacon of his deacon, the nutshell of the nutshell."

What patriarch was he talking about? They grew impatient and they did not ask him. They let him calm down.

"Do you agree, wife?"

"Of course I agree."

Papa-Vasilis did not like the "of course" part, which was also redundant (you became one with them, wife).

"Okay," he said, "I'll go, don't worry."

And papa-Vasilis went, with the difference that he had another idea and, instead of going to Batistas, he went to Antonellos.

"My dear Antonellos, this and this is going on. Talk to your father."

Antonellos' answer came quick and resolute:

He would not allow a mosque to be built at the estate. He would take care of it.

Papa-Vasilis did not expect such an immediate assurance, and he passed it by.

"So, will you talk to your father? He always does what you ask him to."

"Tell the village," repeated Antonellos intensely, "that no mosque will be built! Do we have to say the same thing twice, my priest?"

"Have God's blessing, my child," whispered papa-Vasilis with admiration and with something like terror. "I knew it. It was God's instruction to come to you."

Naïve that the priest was, he gave Antonellos' message.

"You talked to the little boy, my priest?" said the Protochorians sarcastically. "What can we say anymore? And what did he say about the hodja's visits?"

"He said that it's difficult to stop the hodja."

"Why is it difficult?" someone asked aggressively.

"Go and ask and come back and tell us," answered angrily papa-Vasilis.

The Krasochorians were also worried about the workers who worked at the estate, and they were trying to fish information out of them.

"Does he ever chat with you?"

"About what?"

"About the fact that he became a Turk, why he did it, and such things."

They would sift every little thing that a worker would tell them.

"Exactly how did he tell you that?"

And when the bishop came, they would discuss everything. He would listen to them carefully to please them and in the end he would draw their attention:

"Be careful, for God's sake, don't do irrational things!"

How could they do irrational things with Turkobatistas? Simply those who were not working for him were trying to get farther away, discreetly and slowly. Not to mention that when they were in need, they would tuck the tail between their legs and go back and knock on his door. Batistas would receive them as if nothing had happened. So much so that many people, instead of being happy about it, would not tolerate it:

"We mean nothing to him. He doesn't give a damn, the Turkofrank."

And it is true that Turkobatistas did not care about the Krasochorians. On the contrary, he cared a lot about his wife, kokona-Maria (beautiful and educated and from a distinguished family of Limassol) and his son, Antonellos.

Kokona-Maria knew everything that led to Turkobatistas' change of faith. Her husband had discussed it many times with her parents. She was listening, without talking back. She was praying secretly with the obedience that women had for the master of the house:

"God, help him."

Turkobatistas caught her crying once or twice.

"Why are you crying? Just say 'no' and it will be 'no' and whatever happens happens."

"I'm thinking of the child. Do whatever God instructs you."

Indeed the child was a big problem. The Turks did not care about the women; it was the man who represented the house, the man who represented the family. However, Antonellos was not a woman; he was tomorrow's house, tomorrow's family.

They discussed it with Turkobatistas and listened to his objections:

"His mother will die. It can't be done. It's too much."

The Turks insisted and, much as Batistas tried, he was forced to suggest "as a first step" that Antonellos simply wear a fez when he turned sixteen.

"Bogus business, sior Batistas," said the pasha, "wishy-washy. They will be laughing at us."

And he reluctantly consented.

"*Neyse.*"

Until Antonellos turned sixteen, Turkobatistas would lecture him every day.

"Don't take it the wrong way, my Antonellos. A Turk is born, not made. Were you born a Turk?"

"No."

"What were you born?"

"Half Greek, half Venetian."

"Yes, half Venetian, half Greek," Batistas would correct. "So, can a little fez change you?"

"No."

"The Turks have taken our island, they are the masters now. What can we do? You'll tell me 'what everyone else has done.' No. We are involved differently."

The ceremony took place in the parlor of the mansion with great formality. Turkobatistas was trying to balance the essentially small value of the weird and unorthodox ceremony, the "bogus business," as the pasha had called it.

The parlor was the center of Turkobatistas' silent propaganda, which reminded of the Byzantinism of the emperors. Heavy red damask curtains, enormous carved armchairs embroidered with gold, velvet couches and cushions, a large bronze brazier with silver decorations, here and there mother-of-pearl little tables with carved coffee pots and trinkets; on a glass stand in a corner a small golden nargile, "a present from Constantinople" as Turkobatistas used to say without saying from whom (He did not have to say; a small golden nargile spoke for itself), on the walls paintings with thick frames and a portrait of the Sultan.

The parlor—and the estate in general—had even more glamour, because it was in a poor rural area of a small island with cottages and sheepfolds.

The visitor was bedazzled and defeated before even fighting.

"It's here that I fight," Batistas was telling his wife, "it's with such things that I fight, such things are my fortress."

And he was joking:

"Not to mention that such things brought us also the fez!"

The parlor was very familiar to the pasha. He proceeded comfortably and sat on the middle cushion. He was a middle-aged, fat and short little man with a round face and small, blue eyes which betrayed simplicity and kindness.

Other visitors came in behind the pasha.

Even though "it was bogus business," the pasha was happy and smiling because, however you look at it, Antonellos' little fez was a kind of success on his part, which would be appreciated in Constantinople. It was a kind of continuation of Batistas' conversion. After all, how many other Greeks became Turks all these years and how many children put on the fez?

Suddenly, however, his smile vanished when his eye caught a big painting of a Venetian captain on the opposite wall. Strange, he did not remember seeing it before. He beckoned to Turkobatistas, who ran immediately.

"My pasha! *Emrinizde*!"

The pasha asked in a low voice, almost whispering, about the painting. Was it always there?

"No, it wasn't. I've just finished it."

The pasha did not understand. And Turkobatistas explained that it represented an old ancestor of his and that he himself painted it from sketches of that period.

"And today, of all days, you decided to hang it on the wall, *canım*?"

"I thought today, since it's a big day...."

"So that the ancestor can see too?" the pasha said sarcastically.

Batistas smiled timidly trying to assess the pasha's objections.

Had the ancestor lived in Cyprus?

Yes, so the story goes; years ago, many years ago.

He had never said anything about him, said the pasha.

"It seems that it never came up. Old stories, my bey."

Besides, what would he tell him? Did he know more? Some sketches in a trunk and nothing more. So he made a portrait just to pass the time, he liked it and hung it on the wall. He did not even know his name.

The pasha did not want to take it too far on such a day. He showed his displeasure with a grimace and said condescendingly and at the same time sternly and reproachfully:

"The others see too, *canım*. Do you understand?"

"All right, my master, we'll see. No reason to worry and ruin your mood."

At that moment Antonellos came in with his big, blue eyes and blond, curly hair. He bowed in front of the pasha, kissed his father's hand, and went up on the round platform which was placed under the painting of the "ancestor." He was wearing a silk, white shirt with golden beads and flounce sleeves. His velvet breeches were tied a little under the knee with two bows which also supported his high white socks. Around the waist he had a wide, red belt. His shiny pumps with the big silver buckles were gleaming with a bunch of sun that aimed at them from the window and came and fell precisely on them. On his hand a large, blue ruby.

Everybody looked at him with admiration.

"Your son is very handsome today," said the pasha, "*çok güzel*!"

In the parlor were the notables of the Kokkinochoria, who could not turn down the invitation, the agas of the district, the mufti, and the escorts of the pasha.

As in most formal Turkish ceremonies (who knows why, maybe because they might distract, maybe because they might pollute the formality), so also today there were no women present, so for Turkobatistas the serious problem of his wife's presence was solved, because, however much coaching was done before, he could not be sure about what she, being so emotional and sensitive, might do when Antonellos would put on the little fez.

The pasha was now looking at Antonellos and at the "ancestor" as if trying to figure them out. He thought they looked so much alike that he started doubting that Turkobatistas had painted the "ancestor" from old sketches. He told him:

"Did you by any chance paint your son at an older age, *canım*?"

"What are you talking about, my pasha!"

"The similarities, sior Batistas."

And that red belt that looked like a pistol belt.… And why under the "ancestor?"

"My pasha, if I knew that you would be so upset, I wouldn't set the platform there or hang the painting. I will bang my stupid head on the wall for not thinking of that."

Next to the platform there was a carved little table with embroidery from Lefkara and on it a splendid little fez with golden fringes and meander embroideries.

Turkobatistas saw that the pasha had given up the "ancestor" and was looking at it.

"A gift from Constantinople," he whispered to him ("Constantinople," as always, undefined, anonymous, with its implications).

The pasha paid no attention to Constantinople. In fact, he commented on it mistrustfully:

"What Constantinople? With all those trinkets, there is no fez left!"

And he was right. The little fez was drowning in decorations just as the icon of the Holy Mary is drowned in gold decorations, which interfere and do not let us chat, just the two of us, the Holy Mary and us, which interfere and ostracize to the four winds whatever we tell her, and distort it. (After all, why should there be gold here too? Wasn't its glorification in fairy tales enough? Some day its irrational uses must be controlled).

Then, as if he turned over a new leaf, as if he remembered something and turned over a new leaf ("We'll talk about this some other day"), the pasha gave the sign and the pipes resounded happily, just like children that you restrain for a long time and suddenly you let them run free.

Antonellos, who so far was serious and quiet, took the little fez by himself, a sign that he was doing it of his own free will, lifted it high so that everyone could see it, and put it on. The pipes went running up one octave higher and frolicked, framed by the gambols of the drums.

The pasha applauded and immediately the others followed. Antonellos proceeded slowly toward his father, who took him by the hand and led him to the pasha. He bowed his head in greeting and the pasha kissed him on the forehead.

"*Hayır olsun, oğlum.* This is a great honor for you today."

He cheered for the Sultan and the Turkish nation and the others again followed. The pipes were going up and down like crazy and the drums were going wild.

Antonellos went around the parlor and shook hands with the escorts of the pasha, the agas, and the guests. Finally he came and sat next to the pasha.

The servants got in with the large shining bronze coffee pots on their shoulders, decorated with rosy ribbons. In the festive atmosphere, the pasha forgot about the painting of the "ancestor" and turning right he was chatting in Greek with Antonellos and left in Turkish with a bey of the Seraglio. He had forgotten even his comments about the little fez.

"Very beautiful," he whispered to Antonellos as if not wanting Turkobatistas to hear.

He fixed it a little on him and took advantage and kissed him again, on the cheek this time. He was giving him advice, he was describing Constantinople to him, he was telling jokes, and he was laughing loudly.

In the end everybody went out to the garden. Under a huge colorful tent there were tables with all kinds of food and delicacies. The pasha took his place, settled comfortably, and assessed the environment and the fellow diners. He looked for Antonellos.

"Where is the boy?"

"Where is the boy?" the people around him hastened to repeat aloud.

All eyes were looking for the boy. Antonellos approached, and then asked for permission to withdraw for a little while.

"He is tired," Turkobatistas justified him. "He is just a little child."

"We didn't ask him to do any manual labor, sior Batistas. It's a feast that we are having."

"I'll be back," said Antonellos. "I'll just get some fresh air."

And he went out. He went out and ran to the estate. With three strides he went up the stairs.

"Mother, where are you? Mother!"

He found her closed up in her room crying silently. He took off the fez and hugged her.

"I'll take you and we'll go away, mother, don't worry. I'm growing. Let father be!"

Batistas' wife discerned the danger; she was terrified. She wiped her eyes.

"Put it on for a moment; let me see you!"

"No, mother."

"Just for a moment."

Antonellos obeyed. And the mother buried him in her look, she enveloped him. She got up, circled him to look at him from all sides as if she were seeing him for the first time. She fixed his flounce shirt, she untied and tied again the red belt. She tilted back her head and looked again at the fez, she made it a little crooked. Was this a little fez, was this a Turkish little fez? The truth is that it was getting lost and annihilated in Antonellos' beauty and it was becoming an ornament and nothing more.

"What a little prince you are, my little darling! You changed the faith of the little fez!"

"I told you, mother. I'll take you and we'll go away."

Batistas' wife was terrified again. She tried scolding him.

"Don't say that, Antonellos. Your father knows what he is doing. It's none of our business, it's none of your business."

"It will be tomorrow, mother, it will be the day after tomorrow."

Antonellos went back to the festivities. He sat next to the pasha, who had already drunk a lot and his tongue was loosened when he saw Antonellos again.

"Is he just a little child or is he the 'ancestor,' sior Batistas?"

Turkobatistas bypassed the question discreetly.

The pasha glanced at the little fez. Much as it was evident that he wanted to return completely to his initial comments with the provocative tone and the honesty of drunk people ("You'll see, he will confess one day in his stupor," we say), something was holding him back. Antonellos, as handsome as no one else, was right there next to him. Let him be whatever he wanted, let him be as much like the ancestor as he pleased! And let the little fez be just a fake trinket!

And he closed the subject again with his favorite compromising word:

"*Neyse!*"

"*Neyse*," repeated the others without knowing what the compromise was covering.

The pasha drank to Antonellos' health.

"*Antonellonum şerefine!*"

"*Antonellonum şerefine!*" repeated the others.

Antonellos got up serious, brought his right hand to his chest and bowed his head.

"Won't the women dance a little bit for us, sior Batistas?" the pasha could not restrain himself any longer and asked loudly as if to emphasize his desire even more.

"It's a village here, my pasha; we don't have such things, unfortunately."

"What village, sior Batistas? Now you tell me one thing, now you tell me another; *vallahi* I don't like you today. *Neyse. Şerefinize.*"

As for the painting of the "ancestor" in the parlor, even though Batistas had let the pasha understand that he would take it down, it is not certain that he would not hesitate to do it for fear that he might get more exposed in the eyes of his wife and Antonellos. However, he got out of the difficult position when, going into the parlor one day, he noticed that someone had painted an ill-shaped, red fez on the "ancestor's" head. He was disturbed. Who could have done it? No Turk had entered the estate. He was boggling his mind to find out who else it might have been, but he could not.

He took down the painting and hid it without saying a word. He was trying to read the minds of his wife and Antonellos.

"What happened to the painting, father?" asked Antonellos.

(Are you worried, Antonellos? But I have suspicions about you. Antonellos, what message are you sending me? What are you going to become?)

"I hid it," replied Batistas indifferently. "The pasha was offended. We have to go obliquely."

After some time, when the pasha came to the estate again, he was happy to see that the painting was not on the wall anymore.

"You said it and you did it, sior Batistas. I like you."

"I'm not the one who took it down," said Batistas.

"Then who?"

"Antonellos, my pasha. And of his own accord. Don't tell him anything."

"Why shouldn't I tell him anything, sior Batistas?"

"Just because. Don't tell him anything, my pasha. I know what I'm talking about."

The fez could not separate Antonellos from his friends. And his friends were all the boys of the same age in the village, who admired him for his early upstandingness and his guts, and they loved him because he was so sincere, straight, and proper in all his dealings. He never bragged, he never stood one step higher, and he was always open-handed and generous, ready to run and help. The estate was open to Antonellos' friends, it had no fences. And Turkobatistas was disarmed and always gave in when a child, whatever he might have done, invoked Antonellos. As if he were invoking some privilege, some right of asylum.

"I'm a friend of Antonellos'."

It did not matter if the statement was true or false.

I'm a friend of Antonellos'. That's it; it's over, no discussion. A friend of Antonellos'.

"And who isn't?" murmured Turkobatistas between his teeth, to save appearances. And he would tell Antonellos sometimes:

"Give them papers so that I won't make any blunders!"

"The way we are going, we'll become the Inn of Pantzaros!" he was thinking.

The expression had a strange origin. The story goes that once the people of the district of Morphou complained to the pasha that both in the morning, when they were going to Nicosia to take their "products," and in the afternoon, when they were coming back, they had the sun torturously opposite.

The pasha deemed that they were right. Something had to be done. He thought it over, consulted his learned advisors, and found a solution: He established in Nicosia the Inn of Pantzaros where the people who were wronged by the orbit of the sun could spend the night there for free and return to their villages in the morning!

In our times, the expression "Inn of Pantzaros" has in Morphou the corresponding expression "Fig Trees of Ayios Mamas." There were five or six large-trunked fig trees on the way to Syrianochori which formally belonged to the church of Ayios Mamas and essentially to all the passers-by, influenced perhaps by the tradition of the Inn of Pantzaros. Everybody believed that Ayios Mamas, even though he was represented riding a lion, was kind and gentle and was never angry at people for stealing his figs, as opposed to

Ayios Georgios, who does not allow you to take even a tiny little bit of his rightful things, so much so that people say:

"Your things are like Ayios Georgios' things!"

The funny thing is that one day they thought that for some inexplicable reason Ayios Mamas changed attitude. The conclusion was reached from an encounter of Nicholis the camel rider. It was past midnight, and Nicholis was returning from Syrianochori when near the Fig Trees of Ayios Mamas he ran into a strange and unknown priest on a horse. He got scared.

"A priest at this hour?"

He suspected that perhaps it was Ayios Mamas and that he was checking to see who was stealing his figs.

"Good evening," said the priest.

"Good evening," replied Nicholis in a faint voice.

"Are you coming from the figs?" asked the priest.

The question reinforced Nicholis' suspicions and increased his fear. He did not answer and he spurred on his camel frantically.

"Was he riding a lion?" they were asking him.

"I couldn't tell. But he was definitely lower than my camel!"

About the lion of Ayios Mamas, there is the legend that once the Turks asked him to appear before the Turkish judge in Nicosia, and the saint went there riding on his lion. But when he reached the square of the Seraglio, the lion roared and everybody scattered, the judge and the policemen and the people.

They also say that the people were becoming deaf from the lion's roars and that the saint was very busy healing ears. So he specialized and became, and still is, "the saint for the ears."

The parents had initially no objection to their children's friendships with Antonellos, which helped them actually because Antonellos would sometimes assume the authority and solve some of their problems:

"Shall we ask your father, Antonellos?"

"That won't be necessary. It's okay."

And indeed it was okay. Whatever he did was okay. Instead of being angry, Turkobatistas was glad and proud about it.

However, when Antonellos put on the fez, the parents put their interests aside and started worrying.

"We don't want him to turn our children into Turks!"

Some of them advised their children carefully and with hints. They also asked papa-Vasilis to talk to them in catechism class.

For one more time they put the kind priest in a difficult position.

"But have you thought of what will happen if anyone tells on us? They are children."

The priest's wife took the side of the villagers again and talked to papa-Vasilis at another isolated tender moment. It seems that either she considered these moments the most suitable because her priest was becoming more vulnerable, or, under their influence, she would find the courage and freedom of opinion, which she lacked before.

Papa-Vasilis stopped the amorous behavior.

"Whose side are you on anyway, wife, the hare's or the hunter's?"

"Neither the hare's nor the hunter's. I am with God, my priest," his wife answered back.

Now that she got God involved in it, what could the priest tell her! He got very upset and the tender moment was lost again.

"She definitely doesn't care anymore," he thought with disappointment.

And it was not just the fear lest it should become known that he was holding back the parents from pressuring the children openly. Another unexpected danger also revealed itself. Someone thought that he could say something more to his son. And he told him:

"Didn't you put it on yet?"

The joke was very tasteless. The child got angry.

"One more word, father, and I'm leaving this house!"

"You are leaving? Where will you go?"

"To the estate!"

"What did you say?"

"You heard me. To the estate!"

The father was speechless. And the threat was discussed at the coffeehouses.

"They revolted! If one goes, they will all follow, and then try to stop them! They'll form a front of their own!"

That was the coup de grâce. And papa-Vasilis found peace and took his vacation.

Antonellos' best friend was Manolis, son of Çok Pallikari. "Çok Pallikari" was his father's nickname, which he was using to boast and which finally stayed with him. Çok Pallikari was indeed very burly and bold. He gladly accepted the nickname.

"It's true, why should I deny it?"

And if they asked him why half of it Turkish and the other half Greek, he would answer:

"So that both the Turks and the Greeks can understand!"

(In our times, I encountered again in Morphou the nickname in English: "Very Strong." This was also, I think, an indication of some continuity in the thoughts and feelings of the people. And I am sure that if you asked Very Strong why his nickname was English, he would answer:

"So that the British can understand!")

It was widely accepted that Çok Pallikari had once in Limassol "told off a coffeehouse full of Turks." Nobody knew when it happened or who informed the village and again nobody disputed that. How could anyone dispute that when the village was seeking and hanging from such things? Not even the phrase could change in the slightest:

"He told off a coffeehouse full of Turks!"

(As a matter of fact, "a coffeehouse full of Turks" was beautiful. Just like "a neighborhood full of swallows.")

Çok Pallikari also played the violin at weddings. And it is true that in all the weddings that he "did" nobody dared quarrel and "upturn a chair" or draw a knife.

He was boasting about his violin.

"I play with 'votes,' not by ear and at random!"

Apart from the weddings, you could also find Çok Pallikari at the very opposite, the funerals. In all the funerals, of friends and enemies, known and unknown, in the Krasochoria, Çok Pallikari always followed first behind the coffin with his thick stick hanging from his shoulder and with an almost triumphant expression.

"I will take you all," it said!

And he was probably sad that playing the violin was not customary also in funerals, which would make his presence more obvious.

He would wake up at the crack of dawn, and if you asked him why so early, he would answer:

"What can I do? I have to wake up the roosters so that they can wake you up!"

And if someone who woke up late said good morning to him, his reply was also a reprimand:

"Half good morning!"

Antonellos' friendship with Manolis, who had inherited his father's guts, a different kind of guts, without pomposity and self-importance and show-off, was cemented in an unexpected way.

Antonellos had gone out of curiosity to a wedding where Çok Pallikari was playing the violin. He was sixteen years old at the time. He sat in a corner and was watching the dances. All the girls were glancing at him and whispering. Çok Pallikari noticed that something was distracting from his violin. He saw Antonellos. He stopped and approached him.

"It's not appropriate for you to be coming to weddings. You are still a child. Go back home."

The people got up and gathered around.

Antonellos remained seated. His expression darkened:

"I'm not leaving. I'll stay right here."

Çok Pallikari was surprised. He was not used to being talked back.

"On whom are you leaning and you think you can talk like that? On your father?"

"I'm not leaning on my father, it's on my own hands that I'm leaning! And leave my father out of this, for your own sake!"

That remark had gone beyond limits for Çok Pallikari. A milk baby was humiliating him in front of the people! How would he ever show his face again? And the "coffeehouse full of Turks?" He was weighing what to do. How in the world did he get the idea to get in trouble like this? He could not see a way to back out. He was between a rock and a hard place. If nothing else, it was not easy to go against Turkobatistas. He tried to appear compromising.

"Come on, child, go home. It's not right to stay up all night at weddings."

He tried to take him by the hand to get him up. Antonellos became fierce:

"Don't touch me! Go back to your violin!"

And then the unbelievable happened. Through the door rushed Manolis, furious and threatening.

"Leave Antonellos alone, father, please!"

What was this? Would father and son come to blows?

Çok Pallikari was thunderstruck. He looked around at the people once as if asking them to get him out of the difficult situation. And the people understood and got him out. They took hold of him and pulled him away:

"They are children, don't pay attention to them. Their brain has not thickened yet. Don't get yourself in trouble now!"

"Will you stay?" Manolis asked Antonellos.

Antonellos understood the meaning of his question. They had to think of Manolis' father and his nickname.

"No, let's go."

And they left together.

"You shouldn't have done that," said Antonellos.

"Yes, I should," replied Manolis meaningfully, "for you and for my father and for me. Just think if he had hit you and just think if you had hit him!"

The way the events unfolded, Antonellos was able to reciprocate in a somewhat similar manner. Once at the festival of the Kataklysmos in Limassol Çok Pallikari got drunk and he pulled off the face veil of a young Turkish girl. The girl screamed, there was commotion, and Çok Pallikari disappeared in the crowd.

"He was not a local," those who happened to be near told the Turkish policemen. "It must have been an out-of-town vagrant, an out-of-town scoundrel. We don't know him."

The young Turkish girl was Fatme, the youngest daughter of Kâzım aga from Kolossi, who had come with a nanny secretly from her father to see the festival and the games in the sea. She was a beautiful, unruly girl who was inundated and driven to folly by the unrestrained juices of adolescence.

Kâzım aga raised hell at home. Besides the nanny, the mother also got in trouble, because supposedly she knew about it and she covered Fatme.

The insult was great for the Turkish community too. Mounted policemen went out to the villages to look for the perpetrator, to find out which people from each village had gone to the festival. Tough job, how can you keep track?

In Protochori Çok Pallikari could not imagine how dangerous his daring act was, and he bragged about it:

"I was the one who took off her face veil! I sensed something and I thought, 'Let the festival shine!' And it shone! Like fire!"

"Beautiful?"

"Angel of Mohammed!"

"Mohammed has no angels," they corrected him.

"I'm not talking about up there, I'm talking about down here."

"And how did you suspect that she would be so beautiful?" they asked him.

"Experience," bragged Çok Pallikari. "Even if you imprison beauty, it still talks. It screams!"

"You should wear a face veil too, so that the girl would think that it was a handsome young man who took hers off!" (Really, as I was recording the incident, I was thinking, let it be that Fatme would fall in love with the daring young man and that daring young man would be Antonellos and that she would dream about him for years in the harem, or that they would elope and the world would be aghast, and my novel would expand.)

When the mounted policemen came to Protochori, all the people shut their mouths.

The mayor of the village named three or four old people and a couple of women who had taken *sucuk* and walnuts and troughs to the festival. It could not have been any of those.

The policemen went to Turkobatistas too, because they trusted him more, and they still did not find out anything, and they left.

Turkobatistas called Antonellos:

"Tell your friend Manolis to advise his father to stop this zorba-like behavior, because if I report him, nothing can save him. It's no bravery to fight against women."

Antonellos retorted for the first time:

"It's not against women that he fought, father, it's against Turkey. He fought against Turkey all by himself!"

Batistas was agitated by Antonellos' tone of voice and by the word "Turkey," which he repeated twice emphatically (and maybe as a hint, who knows).

"And what will come out of it, Antonellos?"

"What will come out of it? The slave becomes sharpened, gets prodded so that he won't fall asleep! That's what will come out of it!"

"With vulgarities?"

"With vulgarities too! To balance the other things!" (What other things? What other things, Antonellos?)

Batistas just stood there, staring at his son. What was sprouting in his house, what kind of talk was this even before his mustache could sweat! He said:

"Okay, don't say anything to Manolis!"

For two years, Antonellos was dragging the fez on his head. When the first little fez got dirty and old, Turkobatistas replaced it for him with another one exactly the same, with the same golden fringes and the same meander embroideries drowning the red.

He was dragging it to his gatherings with his friends, to the festivals and the fairs riding on his horse. And in the meantime his handsomeness and upstandingness were growing. And just like his friends, the girls too ignored the fez.

"This here is not a fez!"

They were saying actually that the sailors too were wearing something like that.

"Red?"

"Completely red, like the blood of a hare!"

Antonellos' friends never discussed the fez either in front of him or behind him. They did not even mention it. Only once did someone joke timidly:

"Can you let me borrow your little fez for the carnival?"

Antonellos was not mad. On the contrary he was being given the opportunity to show how little he thought of the fez:

"Of course I can let you borrow it! And whoever else."

And he laughed.

The joker took courage and tried to say about "one more fez." He started the talk sideways. Antonellos understood and grabbed him by the collar:

"Swallow that before I wring your throat!"

The boy started trembling, he apologized and said that he did not really mean anything, and Antonellos let him go.

"That's how you let him go?" Manolis was angry.

He turned and slapped the joker twice.

In confirmation of Antonellos' upstandingness, one day a golden pistol suddenly popped out of his pistol belt.

"A pistol! Antonellos came out with a pistol!"

Some said:

"If he didn't have a Turk for a father, he wouldn't dare carry a pistol!"

His friends became enthusiastic and would hold it and scrutinize it and envy it. Antonellos saw their zeal, he understood the differentiation. He told them that:

"I'll leave it at home. It's not right."

What is he talking about? they protested. Now that they were going to ask him to let them shoot too?

Antonellos thought about it, hesitated and in the end he humored them. Four or five of them gathered together and at the crack of dawn they found themselves in the ravine behind Kakoskali.

It was the first time that they were holding a pistol in their hands and a shiver went through them when they put the finger on the trigger.

The ravine resounded from the shootings. Antonellos—an improvised instructor—was guiding them.

"Are you aiming at the target, as I told you?"

"I am."

"Okay. Steady and shoot."

Something strange and inexplicable overwhelmed them when they saw their strength multiplying. And it was not completely out of naïveté that someone said:

"Shall we raid Klavia?"

And they went to the ravine again, a second and a third and a fourth time. Until Turkobatistas found out about it and hid the pistol. When Antonellos looked for it, he told him how dangerous what he did was for all of them, even for the village. He understands, I think.

"I cannot go out without a pistol. You will humiliate me, father."

And indeed for a whole week Antonellos did not go out. Finally his mother found a compromising solution. Antonellos would take the pistol without any cartridges.

"Please do that, my darling Antonellos," she begged him.

And Antonellos went out again riding on his white horse with the golden pistol popping out of the pistol belt, equally proud even

if it was empty. The girls sighed with relief and his friends surrounded him.

"Where have you been all these days, Antonellos? What happened?"

They suspected and did not ask him again to go to the valley.

The one who suggested the "capture" of Klavia said:

"And I was thinking that we should raid Klavia!"

For two years the hoisting of the fez on Antonellos' beautiful
blond head for his outings and for two years the striking of the fez
at home, where his mother and the "ancestor" were waiting for him.

"Take it off, my Antonellos, so that I can kiss you" ("it" was the
fez, which they avoided mentioning).

And Antonellos would toss it down with the same relief that
we, as children, would toss our tight shoes as soon as we came back
from a long school field trip, or from prolonged standing in the
church of Ayii Omologites on Good Thursday and Good Friday
(four hours in the same place with a first love, glancing secretly at
her).

"If you didn't wear it, how would you toss it like this every
day?" said his mother (If the shoes were not too tight, how would
we toss them like that?).

And Batistas was standing guard, watching secretly, listening
secretly (listening secretly like a little maid with the ear stuck on
the door) and admiring without being seen, to avoid encourage-
ment. He would confess to his wife:

"If I say even one word to him, he will bang everything down,
fez and Turkey and everything we've built. Don't you see what an
uncontrollable zorba son you gave birth to? He may bring down the
whole family needlessly and completely out of the blue. He may
bring down the whole astonished Krasochoria."

Even if kokona-Maria was silent, Antonellos would some day
talk unexpectedly, would some day burst out unexpectedly on her

behalf and his. He transfixed Batistas with a look half manly, half childlike, half angry, half plaintive:

"Why did you do that to me, father? What wrong did I do to you?"

He clenched his fists on his forehead and ran out (not with a manly run anymore, but with a childlike one, completely childlike).

He had disappeared from the world for three days and the estate was upside down, the village was upside down.

"He must have fallen off a cliff," Batistas' wife was lamenting, and Batistas and Antonellos' friends were combing the mountains day and night to find him.

No, Antonellos did not fall off a cliff. He came back one day. He said simply:

"Okay, father. I'm back. Forget about it."

As for me, searching through the events, some two hundred years later, I came to the conclusion (let the Center for Cultural Research say whatever it wants) not to consider anyone but Antonellos to be the ancestor. I identified him, in fact, with our Yiorgos. It was our Yiorgos that he was fore-announcing, I was thinking. The friends would ask me:

"So, what happened to the 'ancestor'?"

"Antonellos?"

"What Antonellos? We are asking about afentis Batistas that you were telling us about."

"Ah."

"What ah?"

"Nothing."

I was smiling inside and thinking, "Imagine if the doctor from Asia Minor were still alive and I got sick again and I went to him to check me."

"You have something inside you that is tormenting you."

"I don't know."

"Search for it."

I hesitate and finally I say.

"It may be Antonellos."

"Who?"

"The ancestor."

The doctor bulges his eyes.

"Another ancestor?"

"Not another ancestor, *the* ancestor."

Indeed Antonellos almost brought down the family and actually much sooner than his father feared.

It was the first summer that Ali Niyazi, the son of one of the agas in the area, was coming back from his studies in Constantinople. And he was coming back with a puffed-up head and a great contempt for the island. Since he was a childhood acquaintance of Antonellos', he went one day to Protochori to see him. Antonellos welcomed him and showed joy. He asked him about Constantinople, about Itati, he let him chatter, he kept him for lunch. Turkobatistas gladly entered the hospitalities and increased the treats.

In the afternoon the two boys went out for a walk in the estate. The talk about Constantinople came to an end and Ali could now show surprise at Antonellos' pistol.

"Nice pistol. May I see it?"

He took it, he scrutinized it.

"Very beautiful. From Beirut?"

"I don't know. My father bought it for me."

Ali asked:

"May I shoot?"

"It's empty."

"Load it. Don't be afraid."

Antonellos was in a difficult position.

"I have no cartridges."

Ali was surprised:

"You don't have any?"

"No, I don't have any."

"And you take it out naked for a stroll? Let's go to the estate and get some."

Antonellos was really in a very difficult position. He blushed.

"No, we are not going," he said abruptly.

Ali looked at him for a moment.

"I see," he said bitingly.

He looked at him again while he was silent.

"And I was saying…."

"What were you saying?"

"Nothing. It's just a trinket, I say!"

Antonellos controlled himself and Ali took courage. He repeated:

"A trinket for the girls! What a waste of gold!"

Antonellos controlled himself again.

"You are taking it too far, Ali."

Ali smiled.

"Well, that's how it is!"

"You are my guest today," said Antonellos. "It's not right. Change the subject."

And at night he told his father:

"Now don't ever give me cartridges again!"

Turkobatistas suspected and was scared.

"Be careful lest we all go to waste, Antonellos! And don't forget that you are leaving in October!"

Antonellos forgot his father's advice when he met Ali again a few days later. He was with his friends when Ali passed by. He held back the horse. He greeted Antonellos and ignored the others. Antonellos was surprised to see him again in Protochori.

"Just strolling," Ali said.

And he got down. He shook hands with Antonellos. The others might as well have not been there.

"Did you go by the estate?" asked Antonellos offended.

"No."

"Do you want to go?"

Ali was sarcastic:

"Where will you leave your group?"

"They are my friends."

"Ah."

"What ah? My friends!"

"I don't know. You are not like them anymore."

Them? Who is them? A dark cloud of anger enveloped Antonellos.

"Come on now, don't fire up, and toughness doesn't go with your trinket!" Ali bit him.

"Snake!" whispered Antonellos. "I can't stand you. Your tongue is poison."

He threw the fez down as if to free his hands, as if to get them back. And they were free, and they came back!

"All of you, leave quickly," he said to his friends, who cried in triumph. "Go home."

Manolis lingered on and Antonellos got mad:

"You too, quickly! Not another word!"

Manolis got scared of him.

The next day Turkobatistas went to Koidani to find Niyazi aga.

"It's very serious, sior Batistas," said the aga frowning. "I respect you a lot, and I don't know what to do."

Mostly, he said, it's that he threw down the fez, *canım*, and the others were watching, and there was a big commotion and the villages found out about it too.

Turkobatistas tried as much as he could to justify his son. They are boys, they fire up. He did not throw the fez down; he just took it off so that he could fight.

"I'm telling you that he loves your Ali, my bey. You should have seen how happy he was the first time Ali came to the estate. Leave it to me."

Slowly the aga mellowed down. He did not even know what might come out of it if he took it too far. The pasha might not like it. Who knows his plans.

So in the end they agreed to reconcile the two young boys. And they reconciled them at Turkobatistas' mansion, and they shook hands and they said *zarar etmez* and *teklif yok.*

"It was just a joke, Antonellos."

"The devil stuck his tail," Antonellos said.

It was October, and the teacher had decided that at this time Antonellos would be ready to go abroad for studies. And "abroad" was Venice.

Turkobatistas had justified Venice early on to the pasha.

"Why Venice?" asked the pasha. "Instead of a 'second step,' now Venice?"

Turkobatistas blamed it on his wife.

"The mother, my pasha."

"And why do you let her interfere, *canım*? You have only one wife and you cannot control her? *Ayptir, yahu!*"

"He will go to Constantinople too, my pasha. Let him first spend a couple of years in Europe so that his brain will thicken a little."

"It cannot thicken in Constantinople, sior Batistas?"

"Well, I don't want him to do any crazy things before it thickens."

And Batistas said to Antonellos:

"You are going to the homeland now, my boy. Go and kiss its soil."

He paused a moment. And he confessed:

"And listen. You get out of the mud and you throw away the fez too!"

This was very unexpected to Antonellos.

"Yes, father. It was heavy! It was sinking me!"

Turkobatistas was proud of him.

"I'm sending a fine upstanding fellow to Venice, I'm sending an ancestor, a Bragadino!"

Twenty four hours earlier Antonellos' friends left to go to Skala to wish him a good journey. They started in the old happy ox-carts of the faraway fairs with the festive white tents and the warbling bells and the lanterns on the belly, going back and forth like pendula and measuring the road.

With Antonellos' departure, the mansion of the Batistases fell in silence. The streets and the fairs were different now.

"However you look at it...."

The boys would not talk.

"Leave me alone!"

And every afternoon that the groom was taking Antonellos' white horse out for a walk, his absence was becoming even more vivid and painful. His friends would see the horse and caress him, the girls would see him and get melancholy.

"Antonellos' horse!"

And they would ask the groom:

"Did he write?"

"Not yet."

With Turkobatistas something strange was happening. He mingled with Antonellos' friends as if he were the same age as they, he invited them to the estate to chat, to tell him stories about Antonellos, stories that he had repeatedly heard before.

"How was that with...?"

"How was that time when...?"

And again:

"Tell us about the face veil of the Turkish girl, Manolis. Antonellos admired your father."

"You know these things, sior Batistas," replied Manolis. "There is something else that you don't know."

"What's that?" asked Batistas thirstily, without suspecting what he was about to hear.

"How Antonellos was burning to see Fatme."

Batistas bulged his eyes.

"What are you saying?"

"He would talk with my father for hours asking him again and again. And my father was flattered and would describe the Turkish girl as more and more beautiful and he would raise her to the seven heavens.

'Not angel of Mohammed, archangel.'

They had become best friends.

'Couldn't you save her for me, so that I would be the one to take off her face veil?' Antonellos would complain.

'I couldn't wait for you to grow up.'

'You wouldn't have to wait. This year, even. Tomorrow, today, now!'"

Batistas was listening worried. Manolis stopped for a moment.

"Am I not doing the right thing telling you these things, sior Batistas?"

He was not doing the right thing? A father should know everything when there may be some danger.

"He didn't keep it a secret anyway," Manolis said and continued:

"He took me to Kolossi three times, and we were going around the estate of Kâzım aga."

Batistas' worry was growing.

"You went secretly from me? And what if they had caught you?"

"Why catch us? We didn't do anything wrong."

"Didn't they suspect you?"

"Why suspect us? There were so many people in Kolossi. It was also Antonellos' fez, you see."

"Thank God that the fez proved useful," murmured Batistas. "Anyway, did you see her?"

"No, we didn't see her even though we went inside the estate too."

Batistas is terrified.

"You went inside the estate?"

"How else would we give the aga your greetings and your gifts?" said Manolis smiling. "Throw them over the wall?"

"I sent greetings and gifts to Kâzım aga?"

"You sure did, sior Batistas. And what gifts! Royal!"

"This is crazy. I have never even met the aga of Kolossi."

"I don't know about that, but, in any case, he welcomed us and chatted with Antonellos, who, in order to prolong the visit, started talking about the Castle of Kolossi, about the knights who built it and about the recipe that they gave to the farmers for making a special sweet wine called 'commandaria,' because it was made out of 'commando.' However, as the conversation was coming to an end, and we couldn't see a woman anywhere, we were forced to leave. We even fished out from the people of Kolossi a rumor that, after the humiliation at the festival of the Kataklysmos, the aga sent Fatme to an uncle of hers in Constantinople."

"As long as she was not watching from behind a lattice," Batistas was thinking.

He started now remembering and explaining why Antonellos kept narrating that most Turks of the island were not pure Turks, but a mixture of Turks and Venetians. As his grandfather from Limassol used to tell him, when the Turks seized the island, some one hundred thousand soldiers settled there, but no women in such large numbers came from Turkey. Besides, while the Orthodox Church forbade marriages with Turks, the Venetian women, who were more open-minded and who realized that the new conqueror was here to stay for centuries while Venice was disappearing and they had nowhere to go, were forced to marry with Turks in masses.

Batistas mentioned that to Manolis:

"It's a Venetian girl that the boy was going to see. Don't get him wrong. He wanted to see the similarities for his studies!"

And Manolis teased back:

"Well, then my father took off the face veil of a Venetian girl."

"He took off her Turkish half, that's okay!" Batistas would answer.

Beneath the supposedly indifferent and half-joking tone, Batistas was hiding the worry that was flaring up inside him. He was afraid of a secret love (like the one I wanted for my novel).

"Unseen love?"

"Unseen!"

"That's the first time I hear of such a thing."

"Such as he is, he won't consider it a big deal to steal the Turkish girl and bring her to Protochori one fine morning, and set us all on fire!"

"Well, but they say she is in Constantinople," Manolis was trying to calm him down.

"Sometimes people return both from Constantinople and from Venice!" Batistas would reply.

"Look at the antics of the Fez!" the Protochorians were worried about Batistas' relations with the young boys. "He behaves like a child."

And one day, the first letter, albeit delayed, came, and the mansion buzzed, and it was received as if it were Antonellos himself who had come.

"A letter from Antonellos!"

Kokona-Maria was kissing it crying and Turkobatistas read it word and full stop, word and full stop, to get it ingrained.

Antonellos was describing the long journey, the ports where they had stopped, and finally Venice, how beautiful and large it was. Like ten Nicosias. And what palaces and what houses and what streets!

So, that's where the ancestors had started from?

"Yes, my Antonellos, from there. From those palaces, from those houses, from those streets. The canals passed by and picked them up, the sea passed by each and every street, by each and every house and picked them up. In no other place in the world did the sea do such a favor, in no other place in the world did it condescend to knock, one by one, on the doors of the houses:

'Is signor Giovanni in? Is signor Franceschini in? Get ready, signor Lazzaretti. Let's go.'"

Turkobatistas was mentally living his son's great moments. And suddenly he stopped. On the last page the letter said:

"However, I did not kiss the soil, father, as you had instructed me, and forgive me for that. The soil of Venice is not mine, father."

"Why, my Antonellos?" Turkobatistas is disappointed.

Antonellos can sense in advance the disappointment and is trying to moderate it:

"I don't know, maybe because so many years have passed and I've become kneaded with another soil in the meantime."

Turkobatistas grabs the explanation, he agrees.

"Yes, you are right, my Antonellos. That's how it is. Many years have passed, centuries. Maybe I won't kiss it either, even if I say that I will."

At the same time, he is still hoping:

"The soil will work its ways, just wait and see that in time the soil will work its ways, and it will remember you:

'Oh yes, the Batistases!'

And you:

'Oh yes, the soil!'

You know, they told me about Fatme, Antonellos. I take that into account. It affects you."

(Yes, the soil, but who misses the island so much in Venice and sings in its old libraries, father?

Ever since I saw your face
I can never stop the race,
Nor free myself from the flame
Your sweet look gave me when I came,
So I leave Cyprus for a strange place
But wherever I go, my angel, my lace,
My heart will always follow your pace)

Kokona-Maria did not even notice what Antonellos was saying about the soil and the kiss. For her the essence was the letter and even not the letter, not the letter as content, but rather the letter as contact. Mothers read by contact, for the contact do they squeeze the letter in the hand, for the contact do they press it on the cheek, for the contact do they hide it in the bosom. In vain did Turkobatistas wait for her to notice Antonellos' confession, to stumble upon the last page even if she were not from Venice, at least to stumble for his sake. No matter how many times she read the letter, she would pass the last page calmly with her ears in their place just like father's horse on Troodos the night that he thought that there were white flakes rolling on the path.

Turkobatistas said nothing at the beginning lest he should disturb her happiness until one day he couldn't hold it anymore and told her timidly, hesitantly, and smiling:

"Did you see that Antonellos feels Venice to be a foreign country?"

She was puzzled:

"You should be glad about that, my husband. How did you want him to feel it?"

Turkobatistas hesitated more.

"I don't know, I would say like a homeland."

And moderating it:

"Half a homeland."

"You are like a baby child, my husband. The soil where you are rooted, the soil where you are rooted from grandfather, from great grandfather, that's what counts."

What was she talking about? What about the soil that his ancestors brought with them? Doesn't that count?

Anyway, when Turkobatistas read the letter to Antonellos' friends, he discreetly stressed the point about the soil. And he would have also gone to the Seraglio to read it to the pasha and show him that, whether Venice or Constantinople, it made no difference, because Antonellos was stuck on the island like an oyster, if not for that "you instructed me to kiss the soil."

"What did you instruct the boy to do, sior Batistas?" the pasha would ask.

No, he could not read the letter to the pasha. He would tell him about it orally:

"An oyster, my pasha, an oyster on the island!" (If I were not afraid of how you might take it, I would even tell you about Fatme, my pasha.)

And time went by and summer came and Antonellos returned. What a day that was for the estate and for the friends!

"Antonellos is here!"

The estate buzzed and set up tables and festivities, the white horse neighed, the eyes of the girls sparkled. And Antonellos was passing out all kinds of presents and little gifts from Venice, watches and lace and decorations and little caiques and trinkets and harmonicas, and he was narrating endlessly, and Turkobatistas was proudly watching:

"Tell them, tell them!"

He had come in an Italian suit and a wide-brimmed hat with a feather, more handsome and more upstanding than ever.

"My little darling, my Ayios Georgios and my archangel!" his mother was saying.

He was no adolescent anymore. Nature had already put its final strokes ("A, here and here!"). And Venice and the studies gave him a different flair and different behavior, a gift from the "homeland" which, it seems, looked after him without caring that he didn't kiss its soil. It looked after him and combed him and sent him back so that he could remind of it.

Turkobatistas was breathing in the message of Venice and was rejoicing and being reborn.

The agas of the area were puzzled when they saw Antonellos without a fez. They were also worried about what the people might say. Hopefully he did not humiliate it in Venice, hopefully he did not throw it in a canal.

Turkobatistas rushed to explain before he was asked.

"That's how Europe is, my bey. It's another world altogether. It doesn't like a lot of differences. In fact, even the priests and the bishops take off their cassock. A plain beard and nothing else. *Kocam* bishops."

The pasha in Nicosia showed the same puzzlement and the same displeasure when Antonellos went with his father to greet him and give him the golden carved little mirror that he had brought him as a gift:

"We didn't stay even at the 'first step,' sior Batistas. We went backward like a crab."

Turkobatistas tried to give the explanation that he had given to the agas:

"Even the priests and the bishops, my pasha…."

He did not succeed.

"They put the cassock back on when they return, *canım* Batistas," the pasha said.

He asked Antonellos about his life in Venice, about his studies. He was taking stock of his increased handsomeness and upstandingness.

"You've become a man now, *oğlum*!"

And he continued condescendingly:

"I say, how can a *çiçek* fez now fit you? Just like the little mirror that you brought me, which leaves the beard out!"

"It's not like that, my pasha. You'll see," replied Antonellos.

"I'll see, I'll see and I don't see, *oğlum*," said the pasha mildly. And, as always:

"*Neyse*."

He looked at Antonellos with curiosity. The more he looked the more he doubted that Turkobatistas had copied the "ancestor" of the parlor from old sketches. His suspicion that it was his son that he painted the way he foresaw him and the way he wanted him to be was reinforced more and more, and then he hung the painting on the wall on the crucial day, a target and a guide.

The village was enthusiastic about Antonellos' hat.

"He is one of us. Our children knew better."

And it was a chance to make papa-Vasilis sad again:

"You see, my priest? Even though he is just a mouthful of a child, he is not scared."

"When your father is a Batistas and a convert and you are nineteen years old, you are entitled to a caprice every now and then," replied the priest annoyed. "I told you before, whoever wants the cassock, let him come and get it."

"Don't threaten us," said the intellectual.

The girls loved the beautiful feathered hat even if, here and there, you could hear timidly and in confidence a second opinion:

"Don't tell me now that the little fez was any less beautiful."

"Ptu, ptu," other girls would reply. "Knock on wood!"

They were the same ones who earlier were saying that it was not a fez and that sailors were wearing the same one.

("Red?"

"Completely red, like the blood of a hare.")

For three months that Antonellos stayed in the village, he gave it a different life and a different spirit. He brought his guitar with him, and he would stay up late with his friends and sing to them love songs from Napoli and sea songs about war and freedom. He would tell them about the canals and the palaces of the Doges and the university and the girls. And the friends listened and admired and desired and envied and narrated again at home to their fathers and their sisters.

"What are you studying?" they would ask him.

"Philosophy."

"Philosophy? Does that mean that you'll become Socrates?"

And he was telling them about some new ideas that were boiling in Europe and that would explode any moment. There was lightning in Frankia, as they say, even if there was no thunder. And something was breaking out in Italy too.

"The world is changing; it's turning a new page."

They were listening to him insatiably, they were asking, they did not understand, and they were asking again.

With time, the fathers, who would hear bits and pieces of their conversations, forgot their initial enthusiasm and started worrying again.

"They cannot be restrained, they skip work to go and find him. However much he is one of us, we don't know with what he inflates their minds. He turned the estate into a den."

The situation with the father and the fez had left some traces of suspicion in them, and the truth is that they wondered how come the Turks had said nothing about the feathered hat.

"Whatever happens, the Batistases will find a way to escape the consequences. We are the ones who will pay for the damages."

They thought of climbing up the poplar trees at night to hear what Antonellos and his friends were saying during their walks. Antonellos found out about it and one evening he said loudly:

"Shall we shoot into the poplar trees to see how many thousands of sparrows are perching in there?"

"We may scare the village," someone said.

"No one will even hear in this deep ravine," Antonellos replied and drew his pistol.

And suddenly a scared voice was heard:

"Don't Antonellos, I'm up here."

The "spy" got down like a wet cat.

"I'm not asking you what you were doing in the poplar trees," said Antonellos. "They don't belong to the estate!"

Ashamed, the "spy" turned to leave.

"You acted as if you were from Klavia!" Antonellos shouted after him.

Antonellos even remembered the old unwritten pardon papers that his companions were using ("I'm a friend of Antonellos'"), and he extended them. One day Yiannis Kalaitzis came to him and complained that Batistas sent him away from work "for the merest trifle."

"What did you do?"

"Nothing, my Antonellos, please!"

"It can't be nothing," said Antonellos. "Anyway, you may return to work tomorrow."

Batistas was surprised to see him the next day at the estate. He did not show it. He suspected what had happened.

"Antonellos told me to come back," said Kalaitzis.

"I know, I didn't ask you," replied Batistas. "We had talked about it. Aren't you the father of…?"

"I have no children."

He had no children? He had no child who was a friend of Antonellos'? Batistas realized what precedent was created by the rehiring of Kalaitzis, whom, by the way, it was not for "the merest trifle" that he had fired.

He did not say anything. And he did not say anything again when a few days later the case was repeated with another worker. He pretended:

"Did Antonellos find you and send you? I had told him."

Batistas saw that he needed a quick decision if the order at the estate were to be salvaged, and he urgently made sure that all the people who had been fired in the past for one reason or another return.

"Amnesty, Antonellos," he would joke.

And to the villagers:

"For joy that my Antonellos is back!"

But Antonellos knew that it wasn't like that.

And Batistas, on the other hand, knew that Antonellos knew.

With Antonellos' arrival, Batistas' worries about Fatme were rekindled. He watched his movements, asked about his excursions, asked Manolis secretly:

"Didn't he ask you to go to Kolossi?"

"No."

"Please, my little Manolis, you must know."

And one day Antonellos asked about Fatme.

"I heard that she stayed in Constantinople," replied Manolis, "and that she married a cousin of hers."

"Don't be sad," Çok Pallikari told him. "I'll take off the face veil of another girl. As long as you have the desire!"

Three months passed, October came, and time for Antonellos to leave again for Venice. Same as before and worse was now the bitterness of separation for the father, the mother, the friends.

The ox-carts with the white tents and the bells and the lanterns on the belly left again for Skala.

And behind the new departure, the mansion of the Batistases fell in silence again, the streets became melancholy, the windows of the girls folded in two and would not open. And again, every afternoon, the groom was taking out Antonellos' white horse, making his absence more vivid and painful. And the girls were looking at him dreamily.

"Antonellos' horse!"

And it was papa-Vasilis' turn to say his word to the Protochorians:

"Are you happy now that he's gone?"

Antonellos did not come back from Italy the next summer. He kept writing that he would come and he kept postponing.

"Unfortunately this summer I won't be able to. Next year, God willing."

And he would not come the next year either. His mother was burning. He blamed it on her husband.

"Homeland, homeland, here's what you did to us!"

"What did I do? I didn't say that I was giving him as a gift to it. Just to see him and return him."

"And the fez? This is where it took us!"

"Don't say that. He threw away the fez, it's gone. Why should he be afraid of that?"

And Çok Pallikari was commenting:

"It's a good thing that I had found him a beautiful girl. Why did they have to send him abroad?"

Antonellos knew their desire and their burning and was trying to console them with more frequent letters. They were loquacious, many-paged letters that said about this and about that, in order to distract and occupy. He even sent them a picture. A real man.

"He grew a mustache too!"

"At the Bridge of the Sighs" he had noted at the back.

"Bridge of the Sighs? What is this Bridge of the Sighs? Couldn't he find another place?"

"It's because he knows that we sigh for him," said the mother and she was kissing the picture and crying.

"Down below is the canal," said Batistas to show that he knew something and to break up the emotion.

In her sadness kokona-Maria did not spare him.

"Really? I thought it was a road!"

In the village they found out about the picture and Antonellos' friends were coming one by one.

"Can I see the picture?"

The girls wanted to see it too, they were burning to see it, even if it was not proper for them to go to the estate. They found another way:

"Can you give it to me so that my sister can see it too?"

They gave it to him, and the picture started going around the village and was late coming back to the estate.

"What happened to the picture?" the mother was worried.

"Some friends of my sister's took it. I'll bring it back to you tomorrow, don't worry."

And he would not bring it "tomorrow," and he would not bring it "the day after tomorrow."

"After the 'bridge of the sighs' it takes the 'stroll of the sighs,'" joked Batistas.

Antonellos' friends were sad.

"The canals won him over."

The canals won him over? No, the canals were not to blame. One day a letter came from Antonellos saying that he had been in love for some time now with a girl, Patrizia.

They were relieved at the estate.

("So it was love?")

Batistas was relieved most of all.

("Bravo, my Antonellos. A real Venetian girl, not half. The mixed-Turkish girl is all gone, Venice swallowed her up.")

He was asking for their permission to marry her.

("With all our heart, our Antonellos.")

He was praising her to them for her intelligence, her prudence, her love for him, her beauty.

Turkobatistas had, with secret joy, the thought that the soil must have worked its ways too.

("It works its ways inside you unbeknownst to you").

The reply left quickly. Let the wedding take place there, it doesn't matter. They would have a second wedding in Cyprus. When is he going to bring them the bride? Let him not delay. They are anxious.

(There go the hopes for my novel to be expanded and enlarged with a love for Fatme.)

Antonellos came the following year and brought Patrizia with him, but it was a different return. The estate did not buzz, did not set up tables and festivities. Turkobatistas was seriously ill and the mansion was deep in grief and cloudiness.

"He cannot walk," his mother told him. "He won't be able to."

"Father, for God's sake!" complained Antonellos. "Were you saving this for me?"

"You see?" mumbled Batistas and was showered in tears.

"He cries with the slightest little thing," said the mother.

She went close to him and caressed him.

"Why are you crying? Is it right to cry on such a day?"

Turkobatistas shook his head. He was looking at Antonellos and Patrizia with the increased, the wide and penetrating and strange look of the invalid, which takes on, as it were, whatever was lost from the talk and the movement.

"Beautiful," he whispered.

And then:

"Whole, not half."

Antonellos sat at his bedside. He told him that he missed the life at the estate, that he longed for it all the time, that he would not leave again, that Patrizia wanted that too. And you will see that he would help him rest and he would soon get well.

With the arrival of Antonellos and Patrizia, the estate half-opened the eyes, lifted slowly the head, became alive again. Even though Turkobatistas' illness was bearing down on it, something else started blowing, and the gatherings of Antonellos with his friends started again, even without songs or a guitar.

"They stood by me as if it were you," his mother told him.

Patrizia looked thrilled with her new life. She was overseeing the estate, she went horseback riding, she was painting.

"Just like in Umbria," she was telling Antonellos.

The village almost forgot Antonellos and turned completely toward the beautiful Venetian girl with the black hair and the almond-shaped, black eyes, the men's clothing, the open-hearted laugh (ignoring for a moment the cloudiness of the estate and pouring forth) and especially the warbling language that, even though they did not understand, was flowing inside them like a strange, cool stream on the mountain. So much so that when she started "stumbling" through some Greek, they were worried.

"God forbid that she should learn Greek!"

Not everyone agreed.

"She will be singing her Greek too. Her mouth has it!"

Even the girls of the village loved her and were not jealous of her and were happy for her and Antonellos. Patrizia, for her part, became friends with them and was going to their houses. They were flattered and were killing themselves to offer her hospitality, to show her their embroideries and the dowry on the loom.

Patrizia was also inviting them to the estate. They were going happily and gladly, even more so because for some of them the old desire had not been extinguished completely and they were burning to see Antonellos. Now they could even chat with him, whereas before they could not even say good morning to him, and they had to enjoy him from far away.

And the fathers were saying just for fun:

"He took our boys, the Venetian girl is taking our girls. Let's see who will take us!"

"Çok Pallikari, I'm afraid!"

The new life of the estate was reaching as far as Turkobatistas' room. Much as it was tiptoeing, he could feel it penetrating and filtering, and he was happy and he did everything he could not to spoil its good mood with his illness. He was trying to explain that to his wife.

"I understand. You don't cry anymore, right?"

"Yes, yes, yes."

Antonellos spent many hours by his side, telling him stories of Venice. One day he found his old feathered hat, and to entertain his father, he put it on. He did not entertain him. Turkobatistas took it and squeezed it on his chest and started kissing it.

"Don't start crying now," Antonellos scolded him.

"No, no, no," stammered Turkobatistas.

And he was already crying.

Patrizia also spent many hours at his bedside, singing her unintelligible chit chat. Who could ever imagine that Venice would come and find him in Protochori to sweeten his death.

"You see? I've brought you Venice at your feet," Antonellos was laughing and was translating a joke of Patrizia's.

"She is asking you, 'Don't you understand anything?'"

Turkobatistas was nodding negatively.

"'What kind of a Venetian are you then?' she is asking."

He had to answer, and he asked for a piece of paper. He wrote: "An overseas Venetian!"

Although Antonellos had told Patrizia about his family affairs, he was always concerned about a visit from the hodja. His mother tried to reassure him:

"He is not coming. He came once or twice at the beginning, but when we told him that visits did harm in such an illness, he did not come again. The pasha came too. He sends greetings often."

The interruption of hodja's visits, on the other hand, gave an excuse to the village to bother papa-Vasilis again with a biting remark and to disturb his vacation.

"Christ healed the invalid of the Bible. Now the invalid is paying him back. The bad run-ins with Mohammed are over."

"As long as Christ does not forget and heal this invalid too," said someone else, and the fun started again.

Papa-Vasilis had got tired of them and did not reply. He only thought:

"God, I have sinned. What sheep you've burdened me with! Didn't you have a better one? Let it have been in another area even!"

The truth is that, regardless of what the Krasochorians were saying before about Turkobatistas, they felt sad about his illness and sympathized with the estate. They remembered what he did for the villages and for many of them separately.

"Let's not forget that."

"Come to think of it, even his conversion may have been for the best for all of us. Who knows?"

Some were shocked:

"Oh come on! You are taking it too far."

"I'm just saying."

They would visit him, and Batistas would show as much joy as he could.

Someone gave the idea of holding a prayer service in the church.

"A prayer for a Turk? Jesus Christ."

However, most of them—including papa-Vasilis—agreed with the idea, even though they were not sure that God would listen to them.

"We will do our duty and if He wants to listen, let Him listen, if He doesn't want, let Him not listen!" said papa-Vasilis. "That's His business."

Antonellos delayed to go to Nicosia and pay his respects to the pasha.

He received him graciously. How was his father?

"He is not doing well, my pasha. So I'm thinking of staying at the estate. I've brought my wife too."

"So I've heard."

Did she like the island, was she pleased with life at Protochori?

"Very much."

"You didn't bring her over so that we can meet her, *canım*."

"I wanted to come and greet you first. Some other time. I've talked to her; she'll be happy to."

The pasha did not mention the fez at all. It seems that he had come to accept it. ("That's what bogus business is. I knew it.")

In the meantime, a big event for the estate and the Krasochoria was the visit of the Venetian Consular, who had found out about Turkobatistas' illness. He came from Skala in his landau carriage. Two horses were pulling it and two more were resting at the back, and at the very top, the carriage driver in a military cap and golden buttons and cords. On his right, proud and wavy, was the flag of the Venetian Democracy.

The village was stunned while the landau was crossing the pebble-covered roads and the driver was blowing the whip.

"Avanti!"

It was the first time that the consular was visiting Protochori. And for him to visit, it seems that Batistas had been seeing him secretly in Skala and had kept up the relationship, even after his conversion.

For Patrizia it was a great and unexpected joy. She was proud of her consular, she went out with him in the afternoon in the village, she was talking loudly, she was laughing.

The village saw her and was puzzled.

"Alone with him. And so much laughter."

The young boys got angry.

"Why not? She is not from the Krasochoria."

Patrizia was showing off to the consular. She was greeting here, she was greeting there, she was stopping to chat, she was dragging him occasionally into a yard for dessert and coffee. And the village experienced a small, beautiful variety.

"Did the consular leave?" they were asking the next day. "He didn't show up today."

Patrizia even went to church. She would not miss it on Sundays and holidays. And with a white scarf on her head, she looked even more beautiful in the semi-darkness and the glow of the candles.

"A painted Holy Mary," the old women were saying.

They were asking papa-Vasilis:

"Why is she crossing herself differently?"

"That's how the Franks cross themselves, first left and then right."

"And why first left?"

"Because they say that first they put a nail on Jesus' left hand and then on the right."

"And why with four fingers?"

Papa-Vasilis had to know that one too. And he answered:

"The Franks say that Jesus' palms were open when they nailed Him on the cross, while we Orthodox say that they were closed, that Jesus was scared for a moment and he closed them. Trivial things."

Papa-Vasilis had to know everything, like, for example, why, on the dome of a church only God's eye (a huge eye in a triangular frame) was painted and not also an ear.

"Only an eye," replied papa-Vasilis, "because God wants to see for himself. He does not trust what we tell Him, He does not want to hear how we tell Him."

"Then why does He have His representative, my priest?"

"Well, we don't tell Him through His representative. We tell Him ourselves. Otherwise, the representative would know how to tell Him!" papa-Vasilis would retort.

Then came Patrizia's first child. For the baptism, they carried Batistas to church in their arms.

"What will you name her?" asked papa-Vasilis.

They told him two names: Maria-Anna.

Papa-Vasilis was surprised.

"Two names for one child?"

"It can be done, my priest, proceed!"

"Well, that's a first."

"Proceed, my priest!"

A naïve old woman said:

"Maybe she is a twin!"

"Anyway," said papa-Vasilis. "Let God choose whichever He wants for His books."

(While I am telling about papa-Vasilis' question regarding the child's two names, I get into the perhaps antinovel temptation to mention a similar episode that took place a few years ago in a village near Skala.

The father of the child was a fanatic communist, the priest a fanatic anti-communist.

"Name?" asked the priest holding the naked chubby boy in his hands.

"Lenin," said the father.

"Eleni?" asked the priest surprised. "It's a boy."

"We know it's a boy, my priest. I didn't say Eleni. I said Lenin. Haven't you ever heard of Lenin?"

The priest held the child suspended in order to think what to do. And finally he decided:

"The servant of God Paul I is baptized!")

Manolis was the godfather. He was shining in his new suit, which Antonellos had given him as a gift. And everything was going fine until the moment when papa-Vasilis (something that nobody expected) made an unforgivable lapse. When he asked the godfather, "Have you renounced Satan?" he turned and looked at Turkobatistas crookedly and boldly. He asked again and looked at Turkobatistas again:

"Have you renounced Satan?"

What was wrong with the priest? Was he showing off to the villagers? Did he want to show them that they had unjustly suspected him in the past of not talking to Turkobatistas about his conversion?

Manolis became furious; he flared up:

"What are you looking at, my priest? Just look in the Gospel before we lock horns in church, with the saints watching us too!"

The presence of Antonellos and Patrizia could not save Turko-batistas. In the spring his condition worsened and became more and more hopeless. The estate was shut and in suspense. And Proto-chori was saddened too. Besides, Patrizia's happy note had been lost from the streets, and it was greatly missed. Together with Protochori, the other Krasochoria also joined in the sorrow.

"How is he? Did you find out?"

"It seems that he is not doing well."

And Antonellos' friends were gathering at the estate to watch.

"What's going on? They never leave his side. As if they were doctors, as if they were little women."

The Protochorians turned to papa-Vasilis one more time as if to take it out on him:

"Should you ask perhaps if he wants to receive the Holy Communion?"

People just throw an idea without thinking, thought papa-Vasilis. And he replied:

"If they call me, I won't refuse."

"Then make sure you get the permission from the bishop while it's still time. It's your duty."

"Yes, it's my duty," repeated papa-Vasilis absently.

That was his last normal phrase, because suddenly something strange and inexplicable started working inside him, something strange shone in his look.

"Are you finished?" he asked abruptly.

The Protochorians did not like the sound of "are you finished." They looked at one another.

"We are finished."

"Well, many thanks, God-scorners, for reminding me of my duty!"

The villagers were stunned. God-scorners?

"Papa-Vasilis, watch your words!" someone tried to get angry.

He did not know that he was not dealing with the old papa-Vasilis. Definitely, he must have talked it over with the patriarch because even his language changed, just as had happened with the

178

Apostles during the Enlightening. Now he was using phrases that he had never used before. He did not condescend to answer to the threat.

"Let them call me, and I know what I'll do. The hell with the bishop's permission. I can give the Holy Communion to Satan, not just a pseudo-Turk!"

What was happening anyway? Was he perhaps washing off the "Have you renounced Satan?" of the baptism?

The Protochorians were listening and bulging their eyes.

"And if the bishop wants the cassock too, I will throw it to the ground, take the Lord, and the two of us will go."

"You will take the Lord without a cassock?"

"Without a cassock, without a hood, without a stole. I will take Him even stark naked, as you have seen me in the river!"

The villagers were crossing themselves.

"You are sinning, my priest."

"Oh brother, you will tell me that I'm sinning? I will take the Lord even in my arms, if you want, God-scorners. And I will be whistling. Do you hear? Whistling songs, not sermons. 'Three monks from Crete and three from the Ayion Oros.' I will take 'the Lord' and you won't believe your eyes. And I'll bring Him back so that he can stand at the door of the church and send away the Pharisees. You, out! And you! And you!"

And papa-Vasilis was pointing at them in a row.

The surprise of the Protochorians was reaching its peak.

"We drove the man crazy," they were thinking.

Papa-Vasilis became more and more daring and said even more:

"And if the Lord doesn't want to go, I'll take Him by force!"

"Christ and Holy Mary," said the old women and crossed themselves again. "God will hurl a thunderbolt and burn us."

"If the bishop…," the priest's wife dared to stammer.

Papa-Vasilis stopped her.

"Cut it out, wife, before I go berserk and yell a Turkish insult at you and the bishop!"

The priest's wife was showered in tears. Yell a Turkish insult at her? She tried to faint, but papa-Vasilis looked at her indifferently.

"Throw her a bucket of water!" he said.

The Protochorians were now looking at him in terror. It was the first time that they noticed what a big man he was. A five-yard monster. He could tell off all of them, just like Çok Pallikari with the Turks. Really, was he always like that or did he suddenly grow so big? It is a good thing that he put up with their teasings for so long and did not beat them up. And to think that he was afraid of the hodja and bowed Christ before Mohammed.

Papa-Vasilis finally remembered the big man who threatened him at the beginning.

"What did you say?"

"Me? I didn't say anything, my priest."

"I thought I heard something."

"Nothing, my priest."

In spite of papa-Vasilis' blasphemous behavior, most people tended now to believe that a miracle had happened.

"And allow God to be humiliated like this?" some were disagreeing.

"His will is unsearchable. Do you think He cares that He will be humiliated in the eyes of the Krasochorians?"

And the "miracle" and the "enlightening" circulated in the Krasochoria and everybody was coming to see.

The way things turned out, it was certain that soon papa-Vasilis would also abandon the term "to call him" and he would go and give the Holy Communion to Turkobatistas whether he liked it or not, whether his family liked it or not. He would force open his mouth ("Hold his hands!") and stick the spoon in.

"And would the Lord like this?"

"He wouldn't have a choice!"

The abuse of power was not needed and the disagreements with the Lord were avoided, because they did call papa-Vasilis. Antonellos himself came to summon him. And papa-Vasilis responded with the willingness and the phraseology of an available coffeehouse owner when you order coffee from him:

"Coming right up. With pleasure and right away. I'll take the Lord and we are coming."

He put on his stole, took the Holy Chalice and proceeded erect (not five, ten yards) and proud as if he were going to battle.

The villagers admired him. The coffeehouse closed and everybody came out to greet the Lord, who was passing by. The men bowed their heads, the women knelt wherever they happened to be and crossed their foreheads and the chests.

They always welcomed the Lord with respect if He ever passed by for the Holy Communion of a dying person, but today it was something else. The Lord was going to rout Mohammed. And He was in good hands.

"Grant victories against barbarians," an old woman whispered trembling with emotion.

"Many thanks to you too," said papa-Vasilis without considering that he was holding the Holy Chalice.

As a matter of fact, the old woman could have used another phrase because "against barbarians" reminded, at a completely inappropriate moment, of the phrase "we are going against barbarians," meaning "the river is carrying us away."

"Did I have an intuition when I was asking, 'Have you renounced Satan?'" papa-Vasilis was bragging quietly.

"Look, he is chatting with the Holy Chalice!" said someone.

The miraculous change of papa-Vasilis was needed because now a big chasm was opening up for him, for the estate, and for the village.

181

A week after the Holy Communion, Turkobatistas died. He left his last breath quietly with a last, wilted, and serene look at his wife ("Did you see that I received the Holy Communion?"), at Antonellos, at Patrizia, and at his elderly nanny who, despite her years, was at his bedside day and night during his final difficult days and was smiling at him and caressing him ("Did you think that I wouldn't come back?").

Three days earlier the hodja had also come, and he was kneeling and praying in the next room for Turkobatistas' soul. The estate put up with him.

"Who cares? Let him say as many prayers to Allah as he wants."

They did not let him go into the room of the dying one, though. He gets upset, he can't take it, they explained. Besides, they did not know if he had found out that Batistas had received the Holy Communion, and they did not think it was necessary to tell him now.

Just to be on the safe side, the hodja came with a sergeant and three policemen. And the aga of Koidani was waiting for a message from him, said the hodja, so that he could come to the funeral. Did they notify the Seraglio?

Now that the hodja brought into the picture the aga and the Seraglio, they had to talk to him. And Antonellos talked to him:

"Listen, my hodja, there won't be a Turkish funeral. My father became Christian again. Clean business."

The hodja thought that he could rely on the policemen, and he got angry and shouted that they were lying to him and tried to go into Batistas' room.

"If you know what's good for you, don't take another step!" Antonellos said in a hoarse and muffled voice.

The hodja glanced around, saw Antonellos' friends watching for afar, saw the black fuzziness in Antonellos' look and did not stretch the rope. He said that he would send a question to Koidani. Could he stay tonight at the estate?

The same day Turkobatistas died. They would bury him the next day.

The hodja tried to postpone the funeral.

"There is still no answer from Koidani," he said. "Does the Seraglio know?"

And the sergeant said something in his broken Greek.

"*Nedir bu, yahu*? Did the sugar fall in the water? It's not a *şaka* to allow a Christian priest to bury a Turk. Do you want me to shoot him?"

Shoot him? Papa-Vasilis approached, his ten yards stretched up to the sky, Antonellos and his friends lifted the coffin in their hands up to the sky, and they started.

"Let's go!"

And behind them the crowd, triumphant, followed.

Papa-Vasilis threw a despised look at the hodja and started an early sermon:

"Listen to my voice, Lord...."

"Will he do the ceremony in the street?" wondered the people.

"He is piquing the hodja."

Papa-Vasilis continued as loudly as he could:

"The blameless in the way, hallelujah...."

(If the "teacher" from Pano Pervolia were there, he might say about the "blameless in the way":

"You see, they provided for a case of a funeral taking place on the way.")

And papa-Vasilis would add quietly, to reassure the people:

"I will say it to him also in church!"

Then about the hodja:

"What a waste of prayers to the Allah!"

Ah, if only the slaughtered patriarch would appear suddenly.

"Welcome, All-Holy one. Sit down and listen. You won't believe your eyes!"

On the other hand, when he saw the Turkish policemen watching gloomily, he found a way amid the incense to whisper, turning his head lightly toward those coming behind him:

"Protochori is going against barbarians!"

He said it with his old humor, just as when his friends used to tease him when he was leading a funeral procession in the street:

"One more customer! Good for you!"

And he would answer quietly in the blowing of the incense:

"Knock on wood! Garlic!"

A few days later Turkish policemen and the mufti himself arrived to examine the case.

The villagers hid in their houses, watching secretly from the windows.

During the interrogation, Antonellos repeated that his father returned to Christianity when he was in the throes of death and that his last wish was to have a Christian funeral and burial.

The mufti said that maybe he was not in his right senses.

They could not know that, said Antonellos.

The mufti thought about it coolly. Should he look a little farther back maybe?

They called papa-Vasilis.

They asked him if he had been visiting Batistas.

"You'll see that I'll pay for everything," thought papa-Vasilis with the old bitterness.

The strange thing is that, right after the funeral, his miraculous heroic change was lost, the metamorphosis was lost, the "enlightening" was lost, and he became the old papa-Vasilis, whose mind was consumed by the slaughter of the patriarch, and his tongue returned to permissiveness and mediocrity. He almost forgot completely what he did under the influence of the enlightening.

"Did I say that I would yell a Turkish insult at you, my wife?"

"You did. And you asked them to throw me a bucket of water."

"Did I say such a thing?"

"You did."

"I can't believe that, my wife."

"You also said about the bishop."

"Me? I said about the bishop? I will punish you, wife."

The priest's wife was not afraid of the punishment.

"What punishment, my priest; you've sinned so much and you said that you would go naked with the Lord in your arms."

"Did I say naked with the Lord?"

"You did."

Papa-Vasilis had every right to think that, as long as the "enlightening" needed him, it supported him and encouraged him, and when its work was done, it abandoned him and did not even turn back to look at him. Would it care about a priest, a nutshell? How sad; even the "enlightenings' have fallen off. They did not even wait for him to confront the mufti. Since that is how things were, he could look after his own interests and forget that the Gospel forbade lying. He replied to the mufti:

"Why should I go, my master? He was not my sheep anymore. How could I get into someone else's fold?"

"Come on now, we communicate, you and I," said the mufti.

"Well, I'm telling you the truth, my master."

The villagers had shrunk in their houses. They had shrunk, but at the same time they were sleepless and on guard, because it was rumored that the Turks would exhume the dead and bury him in the cemetery of Klavia. It was not simply a matter of Batistas. It was again Christ and Mohammed ("Don't interfere, he was mine!" And the two of them having a tug of war, pulling this way and that way!).

Antonellos and his friends were standing guard at nights at the cemetery. Çok Pallikari joined them at the steps of the little church with a bottle of cognac and cooked sausages and smoked ham. He would start as soon as it got dark.

"I'm going, wife."

It was a kind of excursion.

"You are overdoing it," his wife was saying. "Since the boys are going, why do you have to go too?"

"The boys are one thing, the men are another," replied Çok Pallikari.

And, in his solitary fun, he was remembering all his family members who had died and his friends and acquaintances. And since he could not drink to their health, he drank to his health with a comforting "what can you do?"

"To my health, mother! What can you do?"

"To my health, father! What can you do?"

"To my health, Antonis!" (Remember our fun times, Antonis? I continue them. What can you do?)

"To my health, holy all! I brought you all. Cheers to you. What can you do?"

With Antonis, the tailor, whom Çok Pallikari mentioned specifically, he was inseparable. One night he said:

"Tomorrow I'll drink the bottle at your grave, Antonis, to remember the good old times. You on the inside and me on the outside."

And indeed Çok Pallikari spread his legs at the grave of his unforgettable friend and started drinking with his usual phrase.

"Eviva first."

And again "eviva first." Always "eviva first" even if it was the tenth glass.

However, leisure encouraged the others to tease Çok Pallikari and someone crawled secretly and pinned his pants down to the grave.

When Çok Pallikari got up to leave, his pants would not move.

"Let me go, Antonis," said Çok Pallikari. "Don't pull! You'll take off my pants. I'm not coming!"

When the episode became known in the village, it impressed and added to the reputation of Çok Pallikari even though there were always the suspicions that he had felt the pinning of the pants and he pretended that he did not know in order to show bravery and fearlessness. They would tease him:

"Did you by any chance owe any pants to the dead one?"

"I didn't owe him a penny. It was his jealousy because he left and I stayed. He is dead, and he pretends that he is brave."

Çok Pallikari liked the stakeouts at the cemetery so much that even when, with time, they were considered unnecessary and they were stopped, he continued going with his snacks and his cognac.

"We remember the good old days with the dead ones," he was saying. "How didn't I think of it all these years?"

The Turks did not exhume the body. They handled the matter carefully and with self-control. Neither did they turn against the village as papa-Vasilis was afraid, maybe because in the mountainous areas their control was loose and they did not want to start any troubles. They left it completely in peace and, at the beginning they did not even bother the estate.

"Did the storm pass?" everybody was wondering with relief.

Everybody except Antonellos. Antonellos was not wondering. He sensed that it was a matter of policy and that the storm had not passed, that it lay in wait if not for the village, at least for the estate.

At the estate, life went on quietly. It was also the big void that Turkobatistas' death had left, even if Antonellos stood firmly on his feet. Patrizia, on the other hand, was not her old self. She would go to the village very rarely to sing her talk and her laugh.

"You are tired of us," they would complain to her at the houses.

In the meantime, the village decreased its relations with the Batistases. Maybe it was thinking that it did its duty, that it was not necessary anymore to take any more risks. Only Antonellos' friends remained loyal and unshaken, however much he would warn them, and they strolled in the evenings at the estate.

"Maybe the Klavians will ambush you."

And they would remember the golden smoked pistol and the ravine behind the Kakoskali:

"We were right when we were saying that we should seize Klavia and finish with it."

Not only the village, but also friends from Nicosia and Limassol, Greeks and Turks, moved away from the Batistases. And the landau of the Venetian Consular did not appear again on the pebble-covered streets, the landau with the proud, bedecked carriage driver and the flag waving.

"Avanti!"

And so two years passed. Some signs convinced Antonellos that the Turks were playing with him like the cat with the mouse.

The property taxes increased again and again, the wheat supervisor gave him all kinds of difficulties, mounted policemen would come every little while and dismount at the estate, and, above all, they took the estate land from Antonellos and gave it to the Klavians, who now got into the estate and ravished and stole and did damages and nailed horrible knives on the trees.

"The estate land does not belong to Klavia," Antonellos was protesting. "Give it to the Protochorians."

Nothing. Nobody would listen to him.

Batistas' wife was worried.

"Let's sell everything and leave, Antonellos. On purpose did they bring the stabbers in the neighborhood."

"Don't say that again, mother. We are not leaving."

With the friends, on the other hand, he had a different problem. They were saying to him:

"If we let the Klavians, they will eat up both the estate and the village."

Antonellos was holding them back. He would repeat his father's phrase:

"Leave that; that's my business."

And he went to the Seraglio to see the pasha. He returned two days later.

"He didn't see me."

"What happens now?"

"We will make them not dare come here."

They were devising and studying their plan carefully. Nothing should be done on the estate land, so that the village would not get in trouble. It had to be out on the road, where they come and go. And nothing should show. They should just disappear, as if the ground opened up and swallowed them. No foot prints, no traces, nothing. *Kayboldu.*

They did not have time to put their plan into action. One day, as Antonellos was passing by the square of the village, he suddenly ran into Ali Niyazi riding on his horse. He had not seen him in years. He had become a strong, tall Turk. Antonellos greeted him pleasantly.

"*Hoş geldin, Ali Bey. Buyurun.*"

"*Hoş buldum,*" replied Ali coolly.

"*Ne haber*? Where have you been all this time?"

Ali did not answer.

"I went by the estate and didn't find you," he said.

"Really? I'm sorry. Get down and have some coffee."

"I wanted to talk to you," continued Ali in the same cool tone.

"Yes? Tell me."

Some curious people stood by and watched.

Ali took slowly a big, dirty fez out of the saddle bag, bent down, and put it on Antonellos' head.

"You forgot this in a whorehouse in Venice!"

The blood went rushing and burning up to Antonellos' head. His eyes clouded. The curious ones drew away frightened.

"What did you say, you rotten bastard?"

Ali took out one more fez.

"And this one is for the grave of Turkobatistas, your father."

He started to leave. He did not make it. Antonellos jumped like lightning on the horse and threw him down. He started hitting his head like crazy on the pavement.

"I don't want to dirty a knife, you miserable scumbag."

The people who gathered were scared; they did not dare come near.

"Don't, Antonellos. Think of your mother, your wife, the child."

When Antonellos recovered, it was too late. Ali stayed lying down with his face stuck in the rocks.

"Run, Antonellos, they will hang you."

The people scattered like ants and the square became empty at once. No one was left except Antonellos, looking silently at the dead man. He whispered:

"He dared by himself like Çok Pallikari!"

Then he brought other things in mind:

"Forgive me, father, I didn't make it to the end."

The stories say that Antonellos with his mother, Patrizia, and the child went to the Venetian Consulate in Skala and they even say that the pasha closed his eyes, and the family left for Misr. The pasha remembered his friendships with Turkobatistas ("Even though he made a big mess in the end. *Neyse*"). He was also retiring the following month. He did not want to create any problems for them. And to tell the truth, Ali was to blame too. *Hiç olurmu*, were those suitable words to say in public?

In the area of the Krasochoria and farther down, the legend of Antonellos, the legend of his upstandingness, his beauty, his humanity remained alive for many years.

After his departure, the estate was divided among the villagers, but they all left instructions to their children, and their children to their own children:

"The estate is not ours. If they ever come and tell you, 'We are Antonellos' children, we are Antonellos' grandchildren, we are

Antonellos' great grandchildren, great-great-grandchildren,' give them back the estate, it's theirs."

The instructions were going down from one generation to the next like holy and inviolated instructions:

"I bequeath a blessing and a curse, if they ever come...."

Here the string of the story of the Batistases in the Krasochoria of Troodos is cut off. We find the continuation (if it was indeed a continuation), in the plains, in grandmother's stories about her strange great grandfather, afentis Batistas.

"Tell us more, grandmother," we used to pressure her.

We did not know back then about Antonellos so that we would ask about him, only about him, to corner her so that she would leave aside the meaningless safes with the golden liras and tell us about him. We did not know back then about Antonellos, but it seems that it is him that we sensed, it is him that we breathed in grandmother's narrations and we preferred them to father's. We did not know about Antonellos (let the advisor at the Center for Cultural Research say whatever he wants) so that we could ask which folk song sang him. To ask grandmother whether in any closed, forbidden room of afentis Batistas, they had found a feathered hat, a wide, red belt, a golden smoked pistol, a painting of the "ancestor" with big, blue eyes and blond, curly hair wearing a silk, white shirt with golden cords and wide, flounce sleeves. "It can't be, such a big estate, not to have a closed, forbidden room, it can't be." And later:

"What was Antonellos to you, grandmother?"

"Antonellos? Antonellos who?"